Elizabeth Maitreyi

The Samaritan

Published in 2008 by YouWriteOn.com

First Edition

Published by YouWriteOn.com

ONE

A LARGE FIGURE is approaching, bundled up against the wind. A child in a red coat skips to keep up.

I think I'm gay.
I want to sleep with my mother.
My husband's an alcoholic.
My daughter committed suicide.
My daughter, step-daughter, grand-daughter, the little girl next door fancies me and I can't resist.
I like to wear women's clothes.
I can't stop eating.
I wish I was a woman.
I haven't had a woman for five years.
I'm in a wheelchair and I haven't had a woman for five years.
My wife won't sleep with me.
I'm sleeping with my neighbour and my wife wants to watch.
I can't get a girlfriend.
These are the things they tell you.

THERE IS NO kindness in the way the child is hurried along. The child stumbles and is clipped on the side of the head for clumsiness. The distance is too great to catch the words which the wind's discretion whips away. The child is conveyed along at speed by an unyielding grip on the wrist.

My mother hates me.
I hate myself.
I hate my mother.
I hate myself.
My father abused me.
I hate myself.

I can't stop cutting.
I hate myself.
I had no attention as a child.
I hate myself.
My husband beats me.
I hate myself.
I hate my son.
I hate myself.
I saw my brother abused.
I hate myself.
My father killed my mother and made me watch.
I hate myself.
I've never had a woman.
I hate myself.
I never had a father.
I hate myself.
I am abusing my child.
I hate myself.
I am beating my wife and it turns me on.
I hate myself.
My mother loved alcohol more than me.
I hate myself.

These are the things they don't tell you.

Saturday night. 2250

BILLY IS LONELY. *The phone rings three times before they pick it up. 'Samaritans. Can I help you?' That's how they do it. Ring one; ring two; ring three. 'Samaritans. Can I help you?' I like it. It's always the same. Gives me time to get my tongue ready. Doesn't matter what time, always the same. Ring one; ring two; ring three. 'Samaritans. Can I help you?' I like that. I like how it makes me feel. Like hot milk. I feel safe.*

ANOTHER NIGHT SHIFT. *I hope it's a busy one.* On a quiet night the time drags and sleep is near. Kate hangs up

her coat, shakes out her umbrella and signs in. Under the column marked 'Reason for Visit' she writes 'Duty', thinking as she does so about the warm sofa she left behind at home, the late film, the glass of wine. But a call is coming in as she picks up the pen and she moves with three long strides towards the phone. Hearing the phone ring as she enters the operations room Kate moves purposefully, mouthing 'goodbye' to those going off duty, puts herself in the swivel chair, feet on the ground. *Ready to roll.*
'Samaritans. Can I help you?'

WHO WILL PICK up? That's what you don't know. You never know beforehand who will say it. Ring one; ring two; ring three and 'Can I help you?' Who will it be? It's like a lucky dip. Usually I like things to be always the same but some are better not always the same. Like a lucky dip. Sometimes something really good, better than you thought. Sometimes sweets. Sometimes just the booby prize. Like me. Just the booby prize. What Matron called me.

Saturday night. 2350

KATE'S CALL WAS a short one. A lonely lady, elderly, a widow Kate estimates, with panic attacks. A lady used to having someone there. *Too old now to adapt to being alone.* Kate classifies her as a 'nought' on the log. In her mind she reiterates, *Able to tolerate her feelings; no imminent risk of suicide. Nought.* Three stages from coping to giving up. All that separates the nought from the three, is how we manage our feelings. On a bad day, anyone can reach that place where they think death preferable to being with themselves. Their lives stretch into an unthinkable future. Kate ticks the boxes across the page. It reminds her of double entry book-keeping. *Female. Age unknown. Start time twenty-three twelve. Length of call eight minutes. A story that didn't quite make sense - often the case.* Eight minutes' reassurance was all she wanted. *Reassurance when the pills don't work.... or when they do. Will you stay with me? That's what they ask. Will you stay with me? And I say 'yes'.*

THEY TOOK US to the fair at Southport, Matron and the man I didn't like. I don't use his name. And I got the booby prize. We'd come to see the sea but they said the sea was out. Why didn't we come when the sea was in? You don't go to see people when they're out, do you? The sea was out.

THE CALLER IS depressed and I concentrate on feeling my body as I talk to her, sensing into the soles of my feet, my thighs on the chair, my fingers. Compassion. To suffer with someone. We are not here to cheer them up, to solve their problems. We are here to suffer with them and sometimes to provide a space from which to see things in a new way. Which is not to say I don't get fed up. This caller now, for instance. She's one of the 'yes, but' variety. One of those people who hoard their suffering like treasure keeping it safe against all-comers.

AND MATRON SAID, 'Just like you Billy. A booby prize for a prize booby.' They all laughed and Matron made a face that meant she liked that. I felt hot inside and I would've thrown the thing in the sea only the sea wasn't there. The man I don't use his name, patted my shoulder as if he wanted to cheer me up. I looked up but he wasn't looking at me. He was smiling at Matron.

THE CALLER TELLS Kate she doesn't meet anyone.

'My last relationship ended four years ago and I never meet the right sort of men since then. No. I don't go out.' Kate asks whether she has any interests, any hobbies. The caller regards the question as an affront. 'No. I don't have interests. People who have interests are lucky. I don't have any. It's not my fault. I tried all that years ago, joining an evening class and all that but it didn't work out for me. It didn't work out. It's alright for other people. They say to me, Jeannette, you should throw yourself into something - they don't understand how it is for people like me. My life is empty. It's alright for them with their friends and their hobbies.'

There is a slight Irish lilt in the tearful voice. The bitterness is tangible. Suddenly Kate has an idea and asks a question. At first the caller is caught off guard, her tone bewildered.

'My family? Do I see my family? What's that got to do with it? Why are you asking me that?'

Swiftly she moves into outrage and on to the place she knows best of helplessness and misery where her life is Kate's fault. Or possibly the fault of the large family she left back in Eire. *Was there cruelty? Abuse? The father or the priest? The mother going to Mass and looking the other way, offering up her daughter to save herself? Was that it?* Then the anger. 'You know I don't like your voice. You've a very snobby voice. You don't understand what it's like for me. You shouldn't be a Samaritan with a voice like that. You've been patronising me since you answered the phone.' *Shall I ask why she's so angry?* Kate takes that risk. 'I'm not angry. How dare you? My family's got nothing to do with it. You're a real bitch. Oh, what's the point?' *Caller terminates the call. I feel she's probably right. I had judgments about her and that comes across. But if she got to grips with life, would that be letting her family off the hook? Is that why she hangs on to futility and self-pity? Don't feel so good now.* Inside Kate something squirms away from the bad feeling.

Southport. Saturday 3rd March 1973

KATHRYN WALKER'S FIFTEENTH birthday and in her hand she had a flowered mini-skirt in a bag from Marks and Spencers. As soon as they got into town she had persuaded Daddy to buy one. This afternoon her Mum would shorten it and tonight she would amaze the boys at the disco. She was a pretty girl with long legs and long brown hair, still innocent he hoped, but her father was not happy with the skirt. This decision was well outside his purlieu and he had to phone her Mum about it from a call box in Lord Street. Brian Walker, once a soldier, now a solicitor, understood little of the world his daughter was growing up in except how different it is from his own. The war meant he was an old father, forty when Kathryn was born and he is watching the seventies unfold with something approach disbelief. Minis, still popular alongside the midis and maxis, were, in any case, not what he had in mind for his young daughter but as she looked at him so imploringly, he found it hard to say 'no'. He admired out of the corner of his eye the young woman she was so fast becoming - was it only ten years since she sat on his knee? Above the noise of the street he pressed Button A and found his wife on the other end. In a hurry to get off to her sister's, she sighed and agreed to the mini-skirt.

'She can do anything with you, Brian.' 'It *is* her birthday.' 'She thinks *every* day's her birthday with you!' *At least he had the sense to ask.* After the incident with the plastic mac, she had laid down a few ground rules. Saturday mornings they went off to town together, Father to change his library books; daughter to seduce him into adding to her wardrobe. Marilyn Walker was glad of the break. As she put the phone down she looked in the hall mirror and rerranged her hair. Teenage daughters did not make you feel any younger.

Bournemouth. Saturday 8th December 1973

NINE MONTHS LATER almost to the day Kathryn was in a nursing home in Bournemouth, far enough away, her mother hoped, for her not to meet anyone they knew. Mr Walker did not speak as he got the car out of the garage and drove them down there. He had no words for how he felt. The mother-to-be, in disgrace and feeling sick in the back of the Ford Capri, was silent too. Mum, since she found out, had only spoken to her to express her shame and disappointment and to enquire after her physical health. She knew her duty. *Her 'O' levels won't do her much good now.* When Marilyn had helped Kate unpack her tiny case she and Brian drove home. He was patient with his wife's tears as he worried for his daughter. He was more of a father than a husband. *Why doesn't he understand how* I *feel?*

After the marble stairs, girls were shown into a large room with tall, draughty windows and lino. Metal bedsteads and curtained cubicles stood far apart from each other in this dismal place. Contact between the inmates was not encouraged. On moral grounds, what else? This was just as frightening as it had been that night outside the disco. The boy who had seemed so desirable inside with his long hair and crushed velvet trousers, revealed himself now to be much stronger than her and bent on one thing only. He was a good deal older than her and it took her a long time to protest, not wanting to seem silly and unsophisticated. She had never been with anyone who simply did not care, in fact she had never been with anyone at all. A week later she had left a message with his mother - 'Tell him Kathy called'.

Afterwards she realised that this boy had not cared even enough to remember her name. This was more of a shock than the pregnancy.

So William Walker was conceived against a brick wall in the car park behind the youth club, a stone's throw from where his mother lived with her parents in suburban respectability. The nursing home in Bournemouth was punitive, specialising in unmarried mothers. Comforts were few for the mothers-to-be and there was no operating theatre, no anaesthetist standing by, no obstetric expertise. You took your chances here. It was a long labour and an emergency transfer to the cottage hospital was only narrowly avoided. Ten days after admission William put in an appearance, just in time, or so they thought. But there was something wrong. His mother never saw him; they took him away. 'It was a boy,' they told her. *As if he were dead.* When the milk came in and the nurse found her crying, she put her hand on her shoulder and let slip,

'You wouldn't have wanted him if you'd seen him, believe you me, love. Start again, eh? Better luck next time?' She was trying to be kind.

Nine days later the adoption papers were signed and her father came for her on the 20th. Christmas was bleak. Her mother had decided they were moving house. She said the neighbours were talking.

'What about her 'O' levels?'

'She should have thought of that before! Anyway, they have schools in Harrogate, don't they? I can see more of Bessy, she's always wanted us to move closer.'

IN THE EVENING after school, Kathryn has a job at a local old people's home, washing up from their tea-time meal. Often in trouble at school and only tolerated by her mother at home, this routine three times a week is important to Kathryn. It is her independence. She is particularly fond of Shelagh the Irish nurse who is on duty at this time of day. Shelagh is a mother herself but nothing like Marilyn. She finds Kathryn willing and pleasant and they have a good chat whenever they can in the large kitchen as Shelagh prepares night-time doses for the residents and Kathryn dries up stacks of plates and saucers. Shelagh's own children are still young and Kathryn seems an exotic creature to her with her brightly-coloured hippy clothes. Shelagh looks on her as a tropical butterfly that is visiting the home before migrating to a better climate. She lets her clear the plates from the residents' rooms and the old people love Kathryn's cheerful young face. Most of them were young in the twenties and the things she wears remind them of their heyday. They were not children of austerity like Marilyn and Brian..

When Kathryn comes back to work after Christmas, after the baby, it is to Shelagh that she turns - the girls at school could not understand but she knows Shelagh will. Seeing her changed face and hearing her story, Shelagh is moved to tears and takes Kathryn in her arms to comfort her. Suddenly Kathryn, though not a woman, knows something of the suffering of women and something of the solace that the understanding of another woman can give.

Sunday morning. 0012

KATE DOES NOT feel too good right now.

NEITHER DOES BILLY. *Don't feel so good now. Ring one; ring two; ring three. Sometimes I get ready to speak but nothing comes out, just a silly noise. That's just a silly noise, Billy. I put the 'phone down quickly and there's a big clatter. Sometimes I don't even get ready. I just want to hear them say it. 'Samaritans. Can I help you?' If I could talk like them I would be a Samaritan and say that all* the time. *If ever I don't know what's going to happen next or something bad is going to happen, I just call and then I know what's going to happen next. Bad things often happen inside me. That's when I call. Back then, with the man I didn't like, the man I don't use his name and Matron, all the bad things were on the outside. Now they're inside me. How did that happen?*

I CAN'T BELIEVE she did that. Just hung up on him. 'One of those perverts', she said. Why does she work here if she feels like that? One....two...three. Count the rings as you move towards the 'phone and pick up on three.

'Samaritans. Can I help you?' *Being anonymous is part of the heroism. To give all you have and demand nothing. To be the adult who was not there for them. To be everything to someone and yet nothing. Perhaps all they need is to know that someone will listen. What will happen if I don't know what to say? What if they swear at me? What if they don't speak? Is he masturbating? How long do I hold on? What will my colleague think if they hang up on me? How much abuse do I take before asking them to terminate the call? Am I doing this right?*

'Above all remember to ask whether caller is suicidal.' Yeah, actually where do you slip that one in? Mostly you've got a boy on the end of the phone wearing his sister's clothes - 'Can I tell you what I'm wearing?' and a lot of baby oil. 'I'd like you to call me Jennifer'. 'OK, Jennifer, can I just ask whether you are suicidal?' Click. Another satisfied customer. That's another snap then. Mark it on the log. Snap judgment - I don't want to talk to you. Snap, snap snap. Sometimes it's the caller that snaps and sometimes it's the Sam. Only Sams aren't supposed to.

Thursday 20th December 1973. Bournemouth

AT LUNCHTIME THE Parfitts came to collect their new baby. They had been told about the handicap, the operation he would need; they were still beaming when they saw the child and frankly that took some doing. A baby was all they had wanted for years now. At least, Wendy had and what Wendy wanted, Stuart saw as his duty to provide. He would never be the same man again since he discovered his sperm were inadequate, but today he is bearing up and anxious to satisfy Wendy. A deep pool of anger lies buried within.

'Here's your Christmas present, love', said Stuart, handing her the tiny bundle of clean blankets. Wendy had waited for this moment since her first Tinytears, the doll that really cried. Mrs Patterson did wonder about Stuart Parfitt, but of Wendy she had no doubt. This woman had extra love to give and what the child looked like would not deter her.

'And, my God, he's an ugly bugger', said the nurse when they had gone.

Christmas Day 1973. Southport

AN ONLY CHILD, Kathryn dreaded Christmas - it was up to her to make her mother feel it had all been worthwhile, the shopping, the wrapping, the cooking.. And then there was church. Somehow her father was excused but there was always a feeling that Kathryn ought to go and this year was no exception.

'If you don't feel the need to say your prayers this year, young lady, there's no hope for you', said her mother with relish, slapping the mince pies on the table.

MEANWHILE WENDY IS struggling. She loves the feeling of little William close against her, the smell of him, the softness of his head near her face. Feeding is much more difficult than they had told her. Often they both end up covered in milk but Wendy does not care. It is Stuart who is distressed.

'An' it'll be a lot worse when he's on solids!' observed Stuart sponging the Dralon.

Wendy plans to be the best possible mother but Stuart has taken against William. He is jealous. Stuart cracks on New Year's Eve. *After all, we have our routine on New Year's Eve.* Wendy cooks him his favourite meal and wears something floaty and see-through, something Father Christmas has brought her. After that they go to bed. Later when the hall clock strikes midnight, they open the supermarket Champagne (Stuart is an expert) and Stuart goes onto the terrace to light the fireworks he put out earlier.

'You love fireworks, don't you, love?'

This year William brings up milk on Wendy's floaty dress when she is winding him. She has to take it off and wear a jumper. Father Christmas is not amused. Their evening meal is ruined because Wendy has to keep getting up to the baby. Eventually William sleeps in his Moses basket, but when they are in bed and Wendy is wearing her new Christmas underwear, he wakes again. Wendy jumps.

'Just leave him!' Stuart says sharply, 'he's got to learn.' *Learn what?* Stuart gets out of bed and Wendy thinks he has had a change of heart. But no. He puts the Moses basket in the bathroom and shuts the door. Wendy cries too but Stuart does not notice.

New Year's Day 1974. Bournemouth

IT WAS JANUARY 1ST when they brought him back. Stuart was clear, where his wife was in two minds. Stuart held the ugly child firmly against his left shoulder. Wendy sat in the hard chair by the door. The baby looked at her over Stuart's shoulder. Only his eyes were visible. *He looks quite normal.* Wendy hid her face. She knew the rough wool of that overcoat. She hated it against her face, but that was Stuart's way. He never tilted her face to meet his; he pressed it into his shoulder where the coat scratched her face. It was the only way he knew to embrace her.

'This child needs special care,' Stuart told the officer, 'and we're not the people to do it. Wendy's not strong enough and she's my first priority.' *Indeed?* thought Mrs Patterson who was not used to people depositing babies, as it were, on her desk. The Parfitts could not hold on any longer according to Stuart. Because of the holiday, they had not had their Visit. 'Every day she gets more attached to him,' you see, he hissed at Mrs Patterson as if this would prevent Wendy from hearing. *That's the idea, Mr Parfitt.* Stuart went home to his life restored; it was years before Wendy left but she was in time to start the family she longed for.

TWO

KATHRYN IS PUTTING away the crib - her mother liked to get the house clean for the New Year and did not believe in waiting for Twelfth Night Kneeling on the parquet in the hall, holding the tiny plaster manger with the radiant baby in it Kathryn feels her insides contract and fights the emotion arising. She will not let her mother see. Carefully she wraps each piece in kitchen towel and squeezes it gently into its niche in the cardboard box. All through Christmas she has been surrounded by images of blissfully united mothers and babies and the strange paradox of a woman who moves seamlessly and unspotted from virgin to mother without ever passing through the valley of sex. *What was wrong with my baby? Perhaps he needs me.* In the bath she looks at her teenage body which is already springing back into shape. She has no stitches. The wound is in her mind.

NOT UNTIL WILLIAM was abandoned by his adoptive parents did paediatricians thoroughly examine him. It was not just his face that was defective. The lack of oxygen during labour made its effects known to them in due course. Baby William's development was severely affected. By March Billy has joined the other difficult cases in the care of the nuns in the Hampshire countryside. The sisters who served Our Lady of Dolours were kind but distant. Unprepossessing and with no speech developing, Billy was however sweet-natured and no trouble in those days. His operation was shelved. Adoptions were happening at the spectacular rate of five hundred a week in Britain, but Billy was never again taken home. Babies were plentiful; he could not expect to be chosen.

I COULD MAKE some tea. The telly is noisy but I've turned the sound off and the girls are not wearing much. I like them. Time for bed soon. Where's Maeve?

ANOTHER CALL. LIFT the phone. Make the incantation. Listen. Nothing. Mark it on the log. Another call. Lift the phone. Say the magic words. Listen. Silence. Sniff. Small weeping noises. The conversation begins along familiar lines.

'I'm so ashamed.' *Withold judgment. Recover some of the respectful trepidation with which you greeted that first caller.* 'It's difficult to talk about.' *I know where this is leading. Keep your mind open.* 'OK, take your time.' And then you enter someone's own Hell, no longer private as you wander with them through the labyrinth of their feelings and reactions, their self-judgments and crippled childhoods.

And that's why I am here. That's why I put up with Jennifer wanting me to know about his sister's underwear and all the rest of it. Because if I can let go of the things they tell me, eventually they will tell me the things they did not ring up to say. The things they sometimes don't even know. And if they can hear themselves tell the truth, there is transformation. It's a fascinating thing, the truth. Literally. It never loses its spellbinding quality. You can hear it and so can they. There it is hanging in the air between you as if a bell had rung. A beautiful clear sound that somehow changes the nature of the airwaves. All I have to do is listen.

BILLY IS THIRSTY. *Maeve says be careful as I put the kettle on. Don't burn yourself, she says. I am careful. The scars are from that other time when I forgot. 'Oh Billy, you forgot'. I wish she was here tonight. I wish one of those girls off the telly was here.*

WELL, NOT JUST listening. Sometimes a well-timed question can ambush them into noticing how they feel. And sometimes they don't like that; they hang up immediately. You may know they have taken in the question but mostly you don't know anything. If you get it right and they stay on the line they may take a step towards a different life. What kind of ego trip is this? A phone is ring-ring-ringing again. My colleague takes the call. She is what I call in the recesses of my judgmental mind, the wet shoulder. Sympathy is her speciality and the callers love it. Often I feel she is a better Sam than me. But what can we offer those who deserve no sympathy and what good is sympathy to those whose only experience is self-pity? This is the kind of question Kate ponders in the small hours. But then she remembers too those who ring back, those who send notes and donations. 'Thank you for making the difference', 'Thank you for being there', 'Do you remember we spoke last month - well I'm OK now'. So many lives are touched.

I'VE DRUNK MY tea and it's bedtime. 'Wash up your cup, Billy. Time for bed'. I am all hot inside when I think of the park. Maeve has gone now. I don't like the others. I like Maeve when she's nice to me but I don't tell her about the park. We don't talk about my birthday.

ONE THIRTY. ONLY half an hour to go. I'll just wash the cups for the next lot.

IN HER OFFICE Maeve's telephone does not ring and the TV displays its endless round of tragedy and entertainment as she drinks her tea and finishes off the digestives. The ward is locked for the night.

Sunday morning. 0143

TEN MINUTES TO go. God I'm tired.

Sunday morning. 0145

FOR BILLY THE night is long and unknown like the day. His life is unmapped, full of pain and unanticipated difficulty. The compass of experience fails him. His ship is driven by winds of which he knows nothing. Billy does not know what it means to have ten minutes to go. *Inside my head is black and red. Something bad is going to happen. Something bad is going to happen. I'm going to phone them. Ring one; ring two; ring three.*

FOR KATE THE night is about to expand, taking over her life. Oliver who has just come on duty is making tea in the passage. The phone rings. Oliver is 'green', a new Sam who must log in with a green biro and only work with someone more experienced. He does not answer the phone so reluctantly Kate picks it up.

Sunday morning. 0146

'Samaritans. Can I help you?' *Pause.* 'You're through to the Samaritans.' *Breathe.* 'Can I help you?" *I wonder if there's any of that cottage pie left.* 'Take your time. There's no hurry.' *Musn't forget to look at the rota. Oh hurry up!* 'Hello? I wonder what prompted you to call us this evening? Are you having a bad time?' *One fifty.That's enough now. Stop. Allow them enough space. Be patient. Be present. Listen. You're not going anywhere.* Patsy has gone home - 'Say goodbye to Kate for me' - and now Oliver, with his precious tea, is on a call on the next phone. *One fifty-one.* Kate watches the time tick round on the digital display on the 'phone.

'Hello? Can you let me know you're there?' Kate can hear the conversation on the other line. Now Andy, is there too. He is on with Oliver until seven tomorrow morning and Kate smiles ruefully at him as he puts his head round the door and makes a sympathetic face at her across the room. Kate has been a Sam a long time now but Andy is much senior to Kate in every sense. Tall and fit at seventy, he dressed like a younger man in clothes suitable for the wild. Tonight he is wearing walking boots, heavy jeans, a checked shirt and puffa wasitcoat. Left wing, public school, lives alone - if he were fifteen years younger or preferably more, he would be Kate's type and they both know this. He is one of the absolute best among the Sams, demonstrating daily the commitment, the lack of self-promotion, the open-mindedness that the Samaritan movement is founded on. Kate idealises him as she did her father, now dead. Many years ago Andy trained Kate who now turns back to her caller and climbs her stockinged feet up the wall, leaning back in her chair. Adjacent, Oliver is doing his nervous best.

'Are you? Oh, that must be awful for you... No, I'm sorry, I cannot give advice. Just here to listen, yes. Yes, it's always good to know that there's someone to listen, isn't it?' *Still nothing on my line.*

Sunday morning. 0152

SHE'S SAID IT now. If I just hold onto the phone, nothing bad can happen and maybe this hotness in my head will go away. Want Iris. Don't want to think about the little girl. Don't want to think about Iris. If I don't say something, maybe she will hang up. My tongue isn't ready. When my insides are hot my tongue don't work. They beat me for that. 'You will answer me, Billy'. But they couldn't make my tongue work either. Must speak. At seven minutes to two on Sunday morning Billy speaks.

''allo? Can you 'ear me?'

'Hello. ... I can't tell what you're saying.'

'I'm Billy.'

'Sorry, it's really hard to tell what you're saying. Can you try again?'

'Billy. My name is Billy.'

'Thank you, Billy. How are you feeling tonight?'

'My name is Billy and I'm angry.'

'Sorry, Billy. I didn't get that.'

'Angry. I'm very, very angry.'

'Have you been drinking Billy?'

'No!'

'OK. Sorry ... is it difficult for you to talk?'

'Yes.'

'Is it always difficult for you to talk, Billy?'

'Yes.'

'OK. Well I want you to know that I am listening but you will have to be patient with me.' The room is quiet. Something about the tenor of her call has attracted attention. You can always tell when something serious is about to happen. The noise just dies around you. *Oh, God! Two in the morning and I get someone who can't talk. The ultimate paradox. Needing to be heard. Unable to speak.*

But the man has a Liverpool accent and that is enough to stir Kate's exhausted heart. Her memories of Liverpool are fresh in the way that only places visited when young can be. It is 1975 and she is sitting in Lime Street Station waiting for the next train home after her interview at the University. From the window she can just see the Liver building, the sunset in the Western sky that speaks of water out of sight. The glamour of the Sixties still clings to Liverpool like early frost on a blade of grass. Nearly thirty years later Kate softens at the memory. Quietly admiring the definition of her calf muscle - *legs still pretty good* - she walks her feet further up the wall and luxuriates in her tiredness. There is a relaxation into intimacy and self-abandonment at this time of night which allows Kate to disguise from herself the pleasure gained from having her legs discreetly admired by the men across the room. *Er, concentrate.* 'Are you still there, Billy? Why are you angry?' *Oh go away, Billy.*

WHAT AM I doing? She won't listen to me. No-one can bear to listen to me. I sound like a loony. 'Must you make that silly noise, Billy?' That's what she said when I tried to tell her about the man. She hated me, Matron. Now the hotness is coming back.

'Went to the park today.' New words hurt his mouth and make him hotter.

'You went to the....? Sorry, Billy.'

'To the park. The Park. THE PARK.'

'The park, OK got it. Sorry. What made you angry? Was it something in the park?'

'Little girls. Little girls in the park.'

'Uhuh...? What little girls?' *Keep the voice steady.*

'Little girls. In the park.'

'What about them? What about the little girls, Billy?' *Oh God, no. I don't want to know.* Within her there is a contraction, an avoidance, a sense of danger. Kate is tired no longer. She has swung herself around to sit up straight and Andy is by her side, picking up the other headset. He listens for a while and she looks up at him, her face open with tiredness; he squeezes her shoulder and moves away. She is coping. He has faith in her. *Daddy.*

'They're my friends.'

'Are they? They're your friends are they?'

'They're my friends, they are.'

'That's nice, Billy.' *Do they look up at him like this? Pause. What does he want to say? This is not a man you would trust with little girls. Forget the little girls. You have no responsibility to them. You are here for the caller.*

Kate's call from Billy will last over two hours. For the first hour she will learn very little more than that he walks in the park in the morning at the time that children are going to school.

'Is that Sefton Park?' *A shot in the dark.* The student house she shared there looms in her mind's eye. Billy does not think it strange that she knows the park. To him other people are omniscient.

Billy has befriended two little girls who, Kate imagines, tolerate him walking alongside them. She sees him gentle and inarticulate kicking through the Autumn leaves with them. They, testing their power over this man. For he is a man after all and the power that little girls have would corrupt even the angels. *Social services have a different word for this befriending,* thinks Kate. From time to time Andy comes to sit with her, to listen in on the second headset and sometimes scribbles questions on the pad. He directs her time and again to the caller's feelings and silently sharing the burden of her own dread which is collecting like mercury in her stomach.

Sunday morning. 0257

Something about the pace of the conversation is changing. Kate is picking up Billy's words without so much difficulty now and he is growing more urgent. Far from winding down, Billy is growing more fluent. Even so it takes several attempts before Kate can wrest from the syllables of Billy's mouth the name of one of the girls.

'Dorothy!'

'Sorry, Billy. Say again.'

'Dorothy! She's called Dorothy!'

'Dor...?'

'Dorothy!'

'Dorothy! Thank you.'

'Dorothy.'

'OK, she's called Dorothy. Uhuh. And how do you feel about Dorothy, Billy?'

'Don't want to hurt her.'

'No, of course not! Of course you don't want to hurt her.'

'I love Dorothy.'

'That's nice. Does that make you feel happy?'

Billy would like to say 'yes'. He would like to say 'yes' but there is that other feeling for which he has no name and which is stronger than Billy himself, stronger than his love for Dorothy. And with that feeling, that welling in his loins there comes the terrible anger of that afternoon in Southport when the man had tried to comfort him afterwards, after the unlucky dip and the absent sea.

'Never mind, Billy. You and I can make our own fun right here'.

A large figure is approaching, bundled up against the wind. A child in a red coat skips to keep up. The large figure is in a hurry, eyes fixed ahead. There is no kindness in the way the child is hurried along. The child stumbles and is clipped on the side of the head for clumsiness. The distance is too great to catch the words which the wind's discretion whips away. The child is conveyed along at speed by an unyielding grip on the wrist. Billy thought the man was being nice but things had happened then that Billy did not like. Strange sensations and strange noises came at him inside and out in such a way that he could not tell which were his and which were not. He could hear the sea roaring within him. A feeling he hated boiled up within him and yet the releasing of it gave him pleasure which he found over time he could not do without. Billy courts that very feeling he hates, hating himself for doing so. His feeling grows stronger as he looks at Dorothy bouncing in the Autumn leaves, waving to him as her red coat disappears through the gate. Time for school.

'DOES THAT MAKE you feel happy, Billy?'

A LARGE FIGURE is approaching, bundled up against the wind. A child in a red coat skips to keep up.

BILLY REMAINS SILENT. How can he separate the happiness of Dorothy's blue eyes from the happiness of the Autumn leaves she kicks up to delight him? This morning, or was it? she gave him a conker. Billy puts his hand in his pocket to retrieve it and finds something different. The bad feeling starts in his groin and instinctively he moves his hand there. 'You're disgusting, Billy'. He feels the truth of Matron's judgment even as the pleasure comes.

How can it be called happiness when the bad feeling comes with it, is somehow both its origin and ultimate resting place? In Billy's mind happiness is like a wave, the beautiful, white spray of a wave and racing behind comes the dark and powerful energy that creates it instantaneously pounding the beauty to destruction on the sand. This much of his internal reality Billy understands. When the happiness gets in through his eyes and into his heart, his body gets away from him and leaves him dirty and in disgrace just as he had lain wet and shaking on the mud flats of Southport. 'You're disgusting, Billy,' the man had lied.

KATE HAS CAUGHT his urgency in the silence. She is finding it difficult not to harrass her caller; she really wants to know, needs to know. A page-turner of a call. Later she will doubt the truthfulness of all her judgements. *Was my need to hear greater than his to tell? Just good old News of The World prurience after all?*

'So you don't want to hurt her?'

'I..hurt her...don't want to hurt her...'

'No.'

'Just want to touch her.'*Another new word.*

'You just want to? Want to what? I didn't hear that.'

'Want to touch her!'

'Is that a good idea? This is why you rang me, isn't it, Billy? To tell me about Dorothy?' *For I am the elect of God, chosen by Him to confess you. 'You're like a putty saint!', her mother again. Oh fuck off!*

Southport. March 1958

MARILYN WAS HAPPY whilst the midwife was there. The labour had gone well and she was relieved it was over. Everything lay ready for the baby who now slept in the cot nearby. The sewing and knitting that had filled

Marilyn's days lay in immaculate piles in the cupboard awaiting this unknown arrival with no clothes.
Shame to use them really, they look so pleasing on that shelf. They were wool and flannelette; white, of course. In those days no-one could tell what kind of child would arrive or in what condition. Marilyn's baby was a healthy girl - did she feel the prick of disappointment and immediate self-judgment? Did she want a boy? If so she was not aware of it. In her own little bedroom with this capable, optimistic woman in a crisp uniform looking after her and the new baby, order reigned and Marilyn could relax. Sister Braithwaite bustled and pottered as if the words had been invented for her and through the tiny window with its thin flowered curtains, Marilyn could hear the birds. Outside the March daffodils explored the air.

It was a different story once the midwife had gone; for some days the District Nurse cycled by to check over mother and child and Marilyn had a focus to her day, someone to please, someone to appreciate all this hard work that the baby had generated. Showing Nurse how neatly the nappy was pinned, how she was sterilising others, what baby was wearing, how clean she was, this all gave Marilyn pleasure, an identity. She had changed little from the small child she had herself been, waiting interminably to show her handiwork to her mother or her elder sister, eagerly awaiting but seldom receiving the longed-for pat on the head, the exclamation of admiration that most parents regularly produce to honour their offspring's least inspiring efforts. 'That's lovely, darling!'

Marilyn's family were not like that. Exclamations of delight rarely passed their lips; their days were full of toil and shame and worry. Little Marilyn used to despair but soon despair was replaced by toil and shame and worry. She became one of her family. Now, at twenty-seven, she has become a mother and she, in turn will pass on what she learned. The nurse left earlier each day and then, satisfied that Katherine was thriving, her visits grew less frequent and stopped. She could not know that Marilyn only sprang to life when she arrived and froze over when she left. When the nurse stopped coming, Marilyn noticed a change in her own mood. Katherine, gazing blankly from the cradle nearby, noticed it too and, as is the way with babies, she could not differentiate the atmosphere in the room from her beloved mother, nor from herself. She became the anxious, dejected air she breathed; she became the toil and worry that for Marilyn meant life.

There were periods when Marilyn would wonder at Katherine, at her beauty, her good nature and what use would either of these ever be to her? She never failed to feed her, to bath her, to attend to her bodily needs. Yet even as she did her duty Marilyn was consumed by a toxic mixture of unworthiness and an instinct that what she was feeling about her firstborn was not sufficient, not normal; that she was at fault, as usual. This dutiful, distant attention from a mother devoured by her own guilt and inadequacy was far removed from the love affair for which the baby was equipped. This sad facsimile became for Kate motherly love. She was afraid much of the time.

I DON'T KNOW what to do with her. I feed her and change her and take her out in the pram, but I shouldn't feel like this. I smile at people but I feel dead inside. She's perfect; she's just what we wanted, but I can't bear to look at her. I worry all the time that she'll catch something. I won't take her on the bus because there's polio about. If only the Nurse were here. If only Mum was here. Ten miles away but as far as she's concerned I've moved to another country. I couldn't possibly ask her. What, tell her I can't cope! When I met Brian she started being funny with me. She thought I'd be too grand for them at home. Him having a car, us buying a house, that all made her a bit off. She was like that anyway, with me. And now Dad is dying.

IN THE BABY there was resentment too, a huge energy and rage in this tiny form that she should bear the weight of this life-threatening depression, this self-hatred. A furious, savage, internal war began in those moments between Kate's need to live, which grew with her, a need to assert herself, to separate herself from that hideous feeling, and her love for her mother. Kate refused to learn the lesson that Marilyn had learned from her own mother. She was caught in the web of helplessness and rage of one dependent for life on a person she cannot love and yet cannot withdraw from, but she fought back. She wanted more. In time she had more choice. She needed her mother less. She could do more for herself. Loving her mother became so painful, immersing her once more in the self-pity and guilt into which she was born, that she stopped feeling the love for her mother. *Hard to say when.*

For her part Marilyn learned to feel worse each time she looked at Kate. The house she could manage. The daily round of housework, shopping and cooking offered her some satisfaction as she completed each task. But with her daughter, no. However well she made the milk, however perfect the temperature, however clean her baby was, however bright-eyed and smiling, Marilyn could feel better only when Kate was asleep or out in the garden in her pram, when Kate was not looking at her. There was something so demanding in that look, such a penetrating gaze in her tiny daughter, that Marilyn flinched before it. *As if she knew what I was feeling.*

And, of course, she did. Babies are full of their mothers' feelings and this works so well when the feelings are loving and joyful - a virtuous circle is created where the love and the joy is reflected back time and again as in a mirror. It is a less fruitful set-up when the feelings are negative for some reason. When the nurses cooed over the child at the clinic, as they weighed her and counted her fingers and toes, making the baby laugh, Marilyn felt no pleasure, no reflected glory, no love. On the contrary, the more people praised Kate the more she felt a failure, a fraud; the more she felt shame and guilt. *How can I be Kate's mother?*

These feelings too were absorbed by the uncomprehending baby so that she felt no gratitude to her mother who had given her life. She reflected Marilyn's own feelings back to her - that all the good in Kate was despite her mother. The look that the baby turned upon her was no longer demanding. By the time she could talk, Kate fixed upon her mother a look of challenge, a declaration of war. Only Marilyn could interpret this look correctly. Others saw the flirtatious smile of a precocious toddler. Marilyn suffered badly from knowing that there was something missing in her feelings for Kate and the more she suffered, the more she withdrew from her daughter. When Brian was there she wanted his attention for herself so desperately that she could not bear his holding the baby, running upstairs to pick her up if she cried. Jealousy was added to the list of Marilyn's failings and the baby, beady-eyed now, did nothing to dispel that bad feeling. The more her mother withdrew, the more she turned to her father whose love for her was reliable.

BY THE TIME she could walk Kate had perfected the art of making her mother jealous, wretched and guilty. She did not need to try. The more she expressed herself, the more her natural talents came out, the prettier she grew, the worse it got. The more adorable Kate was, the more culpable her mother. Only a culpable mother would not love this beautiful child. For Kate that meant her whole life seemed somehow inextricably linked to making Marilyn feel bad which, in turn, undermined and killed the pleasure in all she did.

She could only feel good if her mother was nowhere near. Only her mother knew how bad she was. Only her mother could see behind the veils to her black heart. With others, especially her father, she felt like the delightful child she was born to be. With her mother in the room they both felt blackened by their relentless, invisible hatred of each other. Each knew the other's secret and each pretended otherwise. Kate learned what her mother already knew - the less contact they had the better she felt. By unspoken consent they went through the motions of their relationship for the outside world, leaving inside a well of anger and pain which threatened to overwhelm them.

Kate was a Daddy's girl and when she started school she found a whole world of adults who liked her, a bright little girl who wanted to please. Her life and death struggle with Marilyn was paused until her teenage years when their rivalry began again.

Sunday morning. 0315

THEY ARE EASY with each other now, as easy, perhaps, as anyone can be with Billy's impaired speech and limited understanding. Kate is in control now and repulses to the far corners of her mind the feeling that this is all about her when it should be all about the caller. She opens her face to Andy and absolves herself as she speaks into the receiver. Andy sees a woman with hair below her shoulders, a once-beautiful face and delicate skin, small hands and feet. He finds her very feminine but he knows she is also clever. He is concerned about her call, concerned for her. Now and again something traumatic happens and you lose a good Samaritan. He doesn't want that to happen with Kate. *Especially not Kate.*

'Is this a fantasy, Billy? Are you making this up?' There is the outraged roar of the misunderstood from the receiver. 'OK. Sorry. It's important for me to understand what's going on here. How do you feel now? ' *That old chestnut.* Billy has reached an important part of his story but there is no calculation in the pause which precedes his next words. He does not know how to do things for effect.

' I got her knickers in my pocket.'

'Uhuh...Why have you got her knickers? ' *Oh my God!* All her fears are confirmed. *Why is that warm rush of confirmation so like pleasure, the spreading heat of orgasm?* Silence. Kate's voice is even with effort. The self-disgust recedes.

'What do you want to tell me? Has something happened, Billy? '

A roar in her right ear. An ululation takes up where the roar leaves off. Kate tunes her voice to an even idler pitch, devoid of demand, of haste, of need and waits for the noise to subside. She caresses Billy with sound, a man whose every utterance is an assault on the ear. 'I can't understand what you're saying if you shout. It's OK, I'm listening. Take it slowly.'

' I bin naughty with the little girl.'

'You've been....?' *Been or being?*

'Naughty! Naughty! I bin naughty with the little girl. I got her knickers in my pocket. I know where she is.' Kate searches briefly for something neutral to say. Even paedophiles, abusers of innocent children need someone to talk to. Even those dangerous lives are worth saving. Over the years Kate has come to understand that she is no different from the most monstrous of her callers. The most violent crimes begin with anger, with a temper no different from Kate's; the most self-pitying callers touch the self-pity in her and painfully she acknowledges it. The great reward of this work is the compassion that can arise for the caller and for herself. *Keep the rythym of the conversation.*

'Was this this morning?'

'Wednesday! My ...' There is a painful pause, '...birthday! Wednesday!' It takes several attempts before Kate can understand these new words 'Wednesday' and 'birthday'. *Is he changing the subject, backing off from his confession? For surely a confession was where we were going?* 'Wednesday' makes Billy's head ache. He cannot remember what it means. *My mouth has done that thing again, My tongue has got into a,* Billy struggles for the word he knows, *pattern.* New words are hard. They make him feel sick.

Liverpool. June 1977

KATE IS PACKING up the last things in her Hall of Residence. Brian is coming to pick her up, as he always does. Her first year at Liverpool has gone well; her exams have gone well, in fact she has won a prize. One in the eye for Marilyn then, but she is proud to tell her Dad. She has a lot to make up to him for.

BILLY IS ON the move too this warm June day. Gladys is having a cry in the larder. The nuns do not keep boys beyond the age of four and the authorities have decided he will go to Greville House in Liverpool. He is four in December and he is going to need a lot of help. They have a special speech therapy unit at Greville House. The committee have decided what is best and nothing Gladys can say will change their minds. In fact Gladys does not get to say anything at all; Gladys is not at the meeting; she is only a maid, after all. Amongst all these women whom Billy calls 'Mother' and 'Sister', Gladys is the one who is really like a mother to him. Her own boy was killed in the war. Billy has to be torn from her arms as she puts him in the car with his small case. The abuse and the speech therapy are on Tuesdays at Greville House in a special room. Matron is very assiduous and makes sure Billy never misses even if he is a bit off colour. He is often off colour on Tuesdays. Sometimes she sits in.

'Come on, Billy, Mr Prentice is only trying to help you. I'm sorry, Ray. Don't know what's got into him. Kids, eh?'

ONLY THE WARMTH in her gut tells Kate that she manipulates Billy and she has her reasons for ignoring that. She is no stranger to sickness these days. Modestly she welcomes each new level of revelation, heralded by seemly hesitation. These pauses are her rounds of applause. Her callers strip for her. Even those shy virgins who have never done it before allow her to undress them. The veils lie around them on the carpet and they know themselves to be naked. *Dammit, this is voluntary work! You do it!* Mentally Kate defends herself against the unknown critic, in reality, her mother. The shade of Marilyn is always with her. She must talk to Sue once more about this. *I'm seeing her on Monday.*

I FEEL SICK. Mustn't be sick. They were cross with me on the coach. 'You're disgusting, Billy'. The pause is what happens whilst he reconciles himself to the nausea.

Sunday morning. 0335

ANDY IS DEBRIEFING her, expertly, gently, thoroughly, as though she were the virgin now, willing but skittish. He allows her to relate her experience without engaging with the emotions it has provoked, without personalising it. It will be in the next relating of the story that they deal with Kate. Right now it is about the caller and Andy is a pro.

Southport. September 1963.

THE HORSE CHESTNUT tree shimmers outside. She can see it through the leaded lights of the sitting room window. Kate is five years' old. Being tested on her tables by her father means she can sit on his knee and share the big armchair. Safe in his arms, his wisdom allows her to relax, to forget herself. Her jealous mother peeping from the kitchen at this love affair is no more than a shadow in the corner of the eye. Her own sense of triumph is an unaknowledged shadow across her heart - there is pleasure here both wholesome and unwholesome, love and vengeance, impossible to separate. She snuggles deeper into the crook of Daddy's arm. He is wearing his old blue sweater; he has been mowing the lawn; he smells of grass cuttings and cigarettes and he lets her play with his special ashtray where you press a button and watch it spin to make the ash disappear. He blows smoke rings for her. When she is sixteen she is allowed to smoke a cigarette with him on special occasions.

Southport. July 1973

MY DAUGHTER. LOOK at her. Much cleverer than me, so worldly. But here she is pregnant all the same, almost as soon as she could be. What kind of life can she have now? Shop-soiled. Still thinks she's better than me, my fault, I suppose, like everything else. Her Dad as daft as a brush. You'd think she'd won a prize the way he's treating her. 'Don't bring your problems home' - that was the message we got. I daren't go out now in case someone asks me something. I never could lie. I think we should move house. I shan't be happy 'til we've moved.

BACK IN THE ops' room Kate's call, of which she imagined she was in control, has unravelled. Her caller is no longer reluctantly unveiling his feelings nor tempting her to ask for more. She is no longer his mother. No. We are talking of the future now, a future out of Kate's control. Billy has made a plan for his birthday which, by implication, he intends to carry out on 'Wednesday!'

THAT'LL BE DECEMBER the tenth. December the tenth. I'll never forget the date. The way they barely spoke to us. Babies whipped away before we'd seen them. They'd never get away with that now. They said it was for the best but it wasn't for my best. Nor little William's. And what happened to him? I never heard anything. I hope he... I hope...he found a nice home.

BILLY'S FRUSTRATION STILL rings in her ear. As Kate painfully deconstructs Billy's language a picture emerges of exactly how he plans to celebrate his birthday with Dorothy. The jam sandwiches under the trees, the kiss in the glass house where he will show her the jungle plants he loves. The removing of little Dorothy's clothes and the lovely dress he will offer her afterwards. Billy's dangerous yet innocent ideas translate themselves as they fall upon her ear into tragedy.

The script is written in every parent's secret place, seared indelibly into the heart by love and the fear which is its twin. The picture is terrifying and Kate begins to fear both for the little girls and for Billy who apparently harbours no understanding of the mayhem his plan will accomplish. Whatever frail structure constitutes his world will surely fall around his ears on Wednesday. Anxiety replaces Kate' s pleasurable and familiar sense of helping. There is a growing sense of constriction as her internal organs have less space. Listening becomes torture as Billy's story becomes clearer. His language, his story as it reveals itself, is like a palimpsest - a layered thing with the horror of the inevitable, bloody outcome lying deeply covered by the veils of his incomplete language, his imperfect understanding of cause and effect. The blood seeps slowly through each veil; does his conscience whisper to him? Kate can already hear prosecuting counsel describe how much Billy understood as he left home with that knife. Premeditation, the *mens rea* for murder, as Brian once explained to her, though he avoided Criminal Law as far as he could. But no-one explained it to Billy. She imagines Billy, blank, his nods and becks and wreathed smiles through his trial.

THREE

'WHAT IF SHE doesn't want to, Billy?'

'I gotta knife.' *Oh Christ.*

'You mustn't take the knife, Billy.'

'Gotta knife.'

'Yes, I know but it's too dangerous. You might hurt yourself. You will hurt Dorothy.'

'Needa knife.'

'Why? Why do you need a knife?'

'Birthday cake.' *Quite. The logic was impeccable.*

'So you won't put the knife near Dorothy?' Silence.

' What if she says 'no', Billy?'

'She's my friend.'

'Exactly. She's your friend. You mustn't hurt her must you?'

'Gotta make her come with me... Gotta take the knife. ' His tone is supremely reasonable.

'You'll get into trouble.'

'Police come.'

'Yes.'

'Police come and put me in prison, Matron said.'

'Yes, they will. If you go around with knives, Billy. Promise me you'll leave it at home.' As he talks she can hear the news broadcasts and see the parents' harrowed faces as they appeal for information about their 'missing' daughters. How many times have we followed this dark story? Every parent knows the words by heart.

> *"Two sisters, seven and ten, are missing from their homes in Liverpool tonight. They were last seen when they left home to walk to school together around eight thirty this morning. They never reached the school, St Mary of All Angels, which is in the Lark Lane area."*

(Shot of the outside of the school, a low modern building surrounded by wire to keep out the fears of the parents. Pupils mill in the playground, their faces deliberately indistinct.) The head teacher, a man you would not trust with your cat, pays tribute to the girls. Viewers wonder whether he is a suspect. We've seen it all before.

"Police are appealing for any information as to the present whereabouts of Dorothy and Polly Brown."

This on the hour for twenty-four hours. At each new broadcast a detail surreptitiously added; their fate more surely sealed. There are limited number of potential developments in the plot. Please use the red button on your remote.

"Police would like to question a man seen talking to ... seen waiting outside... seen driving away... seen behaving suspiciously... wearing a brown coat..."

"A satchel belonging to one of the girls has been found by a dog-walker... found in a dust-bin...found half a mile away... found in her step-father's car..."

"Forensics experts say that the piece of blood-stained clothing found approximately fifty yards... found under trees...found in his possession... found near the bodies..."

"Police are investigating... are holding a man for questioning... are eliminating him from their enquiries... have arrested a man..."

"The body of a ten-year-old girl has been found... has been identified as..."
And then silence. On the television screen the girls appear in their school uniform as if they have not had time to change. Missing, presumed dead by everyone except their parents; their gap-toothed smiles speak already of their untimley passing out of life. Their photos have already the conveniently dated look of the later documentary, the Sunday papers. *"It seemed like a normal Wednesday morning for Polly and Dorothy Brown as they got ready to walk to the school they were never to reach..."* We never tire of reading it.

As Kate listens to Billy, it is bedtime for the missing Dorothy and her sister. Their beds with all the treasures of childhood arrayed on the covers remain empty and pristine. Their parents clasp each other unable to sleep or eat. The mother, Mary, unknown as yet to the public, still wears her make-up and jewellery from another life which ended unremarked around eight-thirty a.m. today. They hang inappropriately on her ravaged remains as on a person embalmed, embalmed by fear and grief. She dwells now in the agony of remorse for the sharp word which sent her daughters hurrying out of the front door, late again. She dwells in an agony of hope against hope. In crises her own mother would have been clutching the rosary, the priest would have been at the kitchen table.

Instead Mary is in a circle of hell where families live with a WPC standing otiose in the kitchen, helping to make tea, open the door, anything to deny the fateful uniform of her calling. And the family collude. They call the policewoman Pauline and ask questions about her parents, her boyfriend; they try to ignore the crackling of the radio on her belt, the smart way she steps outside to speak into it. Or listen. It is worse when she is listening. Murder stalks the known world of the fridge, the cutlery drawer. The presence of emergency in their kitchen twists their intestines and if they smoke, they are lucky. They turn to this comfort and away from food. Food. Can a mother ever eat without thinking of her children?

Sunday. 0254

SHE'S GONE NOW. Kate's gone now. I got confused and she got upset about Dorothy and the cake and the knife. I won't be naughty. I won't. 'Don't be naughty, Billy". It's not like she thinks. You can't have a birthday without a cake. You can't have a cake without a knife. If you're naughty they put you in prison. I think the knife made her head hot, that's why she kept asking, Kate. I don't talk about my birthday. Usually I just do the ringing and 'Samaritans. Can I help you?' and then I put the 'phone down. I should be in bed now.

SOMEWHERE BEYOND KATE'S experience the individual Samaritan offices liaise to make sure that their phone lines are not blocked by manipulative callers. It is not that manipulative callers do not merit help; it is rather that the Samaritans' brief is to be available to as many people as they can. One manipulative caller can deprive others of the opportunity ot speak to someone when they need to. Such a one was the man who called on and off for months during the Summer of 2004 claiming to have taken hostage his ex-wife and child in a house in Leamington Spa and promising to kill them unless the Samaritans could get him on TV. After a call of five to ten minutes, during which he would get progressively more angry and abusive, he would offer to bring his victims to the 'phone and there would be the identifiable sound of a woman screaming and a small child crying. The sounds would crescendo as they approached the phone, the man shouting all the while. Having reached a climax the adult voices would stop their dreadful symphony abruptly and a child's quiet crying would be heard in the silence before the 'phone went dead.

These calls, coming through to random Samaritan offices via the national telephone number, had thoroughly disturbed numerous volunteers. Even taking his call a second time and knowing it to be a hoax was deeply upsetting and eventually the powers that be collaborated with the police to catch the caller. It was discovered that the whole scenario was played out by one man using recordings he had made from the television and for a time he was prevented from troubling anyone new. Those he had already troubled had to live with it. His wife used to call the Samaritans and they failed to keep her alive. After her suicide, he lost his children, he told the judge 'They're there to talk you out of it', he kept saying. To him, his campaign against the organisation was completely justified. They had not talked his wife out of it. But they are not there to talk anyone out of it. Samaritans go with the caller as far as the caller wants to go.

ANDY IS TODAY'S Day Leader and also, by chance, one of the Deputy Directors.

'So you got to the birthday. Then what?' This time they are dealing with Kate's feelings.

'He said Wednesday was his birthday and it was going to be The Day. The Day he was going to see Dorothy again. He talked about kissing her, about taking her into the hot house, about forcing her to take off her clothes.' Her colleagues wait whilst she falls silent and looks blank. 'Oh Andy, he does not want to hurt her but he will! He can't have seen her this morning, I mean yesterday, because it was Saturday and she wouldn't have been going to school. It was confusing. He talked about having her knickers about a conker. I don't know whether he has already done something or whether it's all in his head... Or if he has planned it for Wednesday. What do we do?' Panic, responsibility, grips Kate by the throat. She is sickened to notice that it makes her feel important.

A LARGE FIGURE is approaching, bundled up against the wind. A child in a red coat stumbles to keep up.

There is no kindness in the way the child is hurried along. The child however shrinks as she is conveyed along at speed by an unyielding grip on her wrist.

MARY, THE MOTHER, has entered a new circle of Hell. Her face scrubbed clean of all vanity, her hair secured by a cheap slide, she grips her husband's hand as he helps her to the dais. The appeal for information, the vain attempt to convey the wonderfulness of their children, perhaps only now in loss truly felt to be the centre of their emotional lives, of their marriage. The utter devastation of these people, the man unshaven, the woman bent nearly double with pain provides an unlikely counterpoint to the next programme where members of the public are invited to compete against each other in a quiz. They have the unaccustomed, colour-saturated sheen of ordinary people enhanced by the art of television to look like more attractive versions of themselves.

Sunday morning. 0342

'ANDY, HE'S BOUND to kill her! We cannot just ignore this!' She's shouting. Running his strong brown hand through thick, grey hair he tells her what she already knows, that Billy may well be known to the Liverpool branch as a regular caller, that his story may be a well-worn fantasy, that his story may be something that happened long ago and that she must do nothing. He points out that no-one is called Dorothy any more. Andy's sharp blue eyes remain calm, absorbing all Kate's anger. He rests his hips on the desk behind him as he says,

'You were there for him, Kate.' He leans forward and puts his hand on her shoulder, looking into her eyes as he speaks. *She's not hearing me.* You heard him and that's what he needed. Well done. How are you feeling?' *Do nothing. Tell no-one.* The selection process is very specific. If you are a 'doer', being a Samaritan may be too uncomfortable for you. Non-intervention is the watchword and they are famous for it. It is this certainty which allows desperate souls to call them, to be comforted by them without fear of their lives and their deaths being taken into others' hands. Tonight, Kate cannot hear Andy's 'Do nothing' for the noise of breaking news in her head.

> *"Police in Liverpool have been joined by members of the general public anxious to help trace the missing sisters Polly and Dorothy Brown. They are combing an area of Sefton Park just outside the city centre of Liverpool after a tip-off from an anonymous informant."*

The smiling children frozen on the screen are replaced by news film. A flash of fluorescent red tape through the trees - the press are only allowed so far - men in anoraks bearing sticks, men in uniform, dogs, the ominous whiteness of a police ambulance and forensic suits in the background. These men do not concern themselves with the living. Kate feigns co-operation; she does not need to feign tiredness and with many protestations of feeling fine, she manages to leave the centre and drive home, Andy's home number safe in her pocket, a promise to call him tomorrow on her lips. He has not noticed that she is on duty again tomorrow night and she does not mention it. Nor does he know she is pregnant.

Sunday morning. 0400

KATE ARRIVES HOME to her well-lit, empty house. The larger trees are lit from below and their beautiful shapes raise her spirits whenever she returns home. Her labradors frolicking on the front drive make fake suicide leaps in front of the car headlights and wearily she smiles, and dips briefly into the peace and comfort of her ordinary life. Kate goes in first. *Flick on the light in the hall, kick off my shoes and around to the kitchen to let the dogs in.* They come in through the back door shaking the cold air from their coats, synchronised tail-wagging providing a dumb-show of affection and *joie de vivre.* They are beside themselves with delight that she is suddenly here in the middle of the night and that they can take a break from chasing rabbits, in the warm kitchen. Rob left for Hull four days ago, and the dogs have been alone tonight.

They have been a happy family, she muses. *How many of our friends are still married after seventeen years?* Once upon a time Kate and Rob had travelled together sharing the discovery of unknown cities, each one a rediscovery of each other. When Kate originally returned from Paris with a young, English architect, Marilyn did not hide her delight and anticipation. *So a degree is good for something after all!* She made Rob welcome in a flirtatious way that made Kate cringe. Marilyn's friends heard a good deal about Rob, as if he were Marilyn's own new boyfriend. Kate and her father, raised their eyebrows at each other, as they heard her on the 'phone when he had gone. 'Yes, his father's an MP. Yes, Kate's done alright for herself. At last! Let's hope it's worth the wait.' Her voice had gone up a class. Rob Hurst was quite a catch. Kate had at last impressed her mother who awaited the engagement.

Marilyn was a great believer in engagements. An engagement was the first battle won in a long war. 'You can't get that ring on your finger too early, mark my words!', as a prelude to planning the wedding and an opportunity to size up the future in-laws. She loved projects. It was how she coped with life, living in the future. In 1980 Marilyn Walker was fifty-two and awaiting her next major role : mother of the bride. *Not 'Grandma', not just yet, thank you.* Marilyn had not quite relinquished the glamour of the female lead and 'mother of the bride' was the next best thing. It is playing understudy to your own younger self as you watch your daughter walk up the aisle. The bride of course is trapped in her wear-once-and-shrink-wrap, fabulous dress. *More of a costume, actually.* The bride's mother's clothes, on the other hand, they are the real thing. *Slubbed fabrics, ice-cream colours, the large flattering brim, the still sexy heels. Only trouble is, this outfit is like wearing a placard with your age on.* Middle class mothers, for all their vanity, do at least like to reach the menopause before appearing once more in the aisle.

HOW BEAUTIFUL WE were. A few days' earlier Kate is looking at their photos. *My God, how young. Here is the wedding, the ivory silk, the lily of the valley and the trailing ivy. "Do you, Katherine Elizabeth Walker...?" There's Mum and Dad; she's got that enormous hat and the dress I really liked. Here's Dad in his top hat. Me with a tan on honeymoon, that's Syracuse in the background. I was so thin.* Kate looks down regretfully at her spreading middle but then hugs to herself the thought of Leila. And here are some recent prints, waiting to be sorted. Marilyn last Christmas, shy now of the camera, but still flirting with the visitors. Sebastian and Max, blond and tanned from skiing. Seb, handsome and self-conscious, Max clowning around for the camera.

BUT NO ENGAGEMENT came back then. Cousins were married off; neighbours' children; Marilyn's friends flew all over the globe to witness the joining together of this man and this woman in holy matrimony. But not Marilyn. Marilyn was falling behind. Feeling frustrated, she attacked Kate. Kate felt defensive and grew still more distant from her mother. She also suppressed a growing resentment of Rob himself. In the end their wedding had been a hurried affair without an engagement. Suddenly, in 1981, they got engaged and married within a few months.'You are in a hurry, Miss,' said her mother nastily. 'In trouble again?'

Why do I care what she thinks? But it was to take Kate half a life-time to separate herself from her mother's wants.

Liverpool. September 1981

BILLY IS UNPACKING once more. Eight in December, he has been very fortunate to find a foster family who will take him. He has moved that afternoon to a suburb near the Dingle, a short bus-ride from Liverpool's Sefton Park and the town centre. Fred and Iris Little's house in Stanley Road is big and run-down. One person at Greville House is especially sad to see him go. *After all, if you can't get the words out, you can't tell, can you?* Matron was against the move but her reign was coming to an end; she was overruled. The Littles are a large and loving family, although the children have all left home now, and Iris welcomes Billy like the lost soul that he is. It is the first time a woman has held him close since that morning he lost Gladys. Husband, Fred, has retired at fifty-three on health grounds and he is as delighted as Iris to be helping a young man find his feet. Billy will never work, of course, but Fred lets him help in his workshop as time goes by. Both quiet people, Billy and Fred develop a mutual trust. The bad memories are hidden away in Billy for now. He smiles whenever Iris comes into the room and he likes the way she hugs him a lot. She smells of cooking. A routine is established.

FOUR

Harrogate. 1981

'AM I NOT going to be allowed to see my grandchildren then?'

'Don't be silly, Mummy. Of course you are, but Rob's career is in London. Our friends are there.' Kate is at her father's funeral. 'We can't move up here.'

'It's not my fault we're stuck here in Harrogate. I seem to remember I was happy in Southport once upon a time. Pity we ever had to move.' This was how Marilyn ended any conversation when she felt in the wrong. The funeral was quiet. Brian's relatives were in most cases already dead or too old to travel. His sister came, a difficult woman who had never recovered from leaving the BBC. Back at Castle Hill Drive there was tea and Scotch, ham rolls and Scotch eggs. Marilyn was well looked after. Neighbours and women from the church took over the kitchen and were quietly jolly as they prepared food and washed up. They loved funerals. Jill, Mrs Blunt when Kate was little, took her aside to say how kind Brian had been to her family, how proud he was of Kate, how he talked about her.

Rob was uncomfortable, shifting from foot to foot and doing his best to make conversation with Mr Blunt. When she was leaving to go back to London Kate knew she must kiss her mother - an act that always filled her with fear. A pain like a knife shot through her when she realised she would never again kiss her father, that he would not see her children. Somehow Rob noticed how distressed she was from his position by the buffet table and soon they were safely in the car. The seat-belt will only just go around her now.

The West London Hospital, Hammersmith. 1982

THIS TIME THE birth was a terrifying, glorious, emotional affair of life and death. Twins! As Kate described it afterwards, it was like seeing *The Trojan Women* and *It's A Wonderful Life* in the same afternoon. Kate was completely enchanted with her babies and exhausted with the responsibility of keeping them alive. Marilyn was too busy to come and help - she had a new dog with a skin condition and special dietary requirements. Luckily, because it was twins, the hospital kept Kate in for a week so that she could rest and someone would feed her whilst she fed her sons. *It was about six weeks before I got dressed!*

Liverpool. December 1988

LIFE HAS CHANGED for Billy. His world is bigger now. He has had an operation on his face so that food and speech are easier. He goes to church with Iris and she used to take him to school but now he is thirteen he goes on the bus. He has a new special school near Sefton Park. She and Fred rehearsed the journey with him until he felt secure. The bus-ride is a big adventure for him and he likes to go early to walk in the park. He likes the Autumn leaves and often brings home a selection for Iris to stick in their scrap-book. Billy does not tell Iris or Fred about Dorothy, a friend he has made at the school. She is Billy's age and desperate to have a boyfriend like her sister. But Dorothy is fat with teeth that stick out and the boys are not interested in her. She and Billy get on immediately and they steal time together in the park before school. All is well until Billy's birthday when Dorothy stays out too late and her mother finds out about the friendship. She appears on Iris's doorstep, indignant. Patiently Iris calms her down and promises to keep a closer eye on Billy in future. At least no harm has been done, they agree.

In the late afternoon Billy helps Fred in the workshop and then they all have tea together. Billy and Iris are waiting for Fred to come home from the pub. He is not a great drinker, but it is Christmas time and his old friends have persuaded him to go out for an hour or two. Billy and Iris have had a drink too. Harry and Angela, the grown-up children, have been round to drop off some Christmas presents while he's out.

Iris's silver tree has been up since the first of December, lights twinkling in the parlour window. Nearby a large Santa keeps watch over the presents - a small but growing pile under the tree. There is a dressing gown for Iris from Fred - she has not opened it but she knows what it is; she helped choose. For Billy there is a new jumper, Turkish Delight and a cassette of hits from *Top of the Pops*. He pokes his presents through the wrapping paper. He is excited about Christmas and confused by puberty. His changing body reminds him uneasily of things he would rather forget. New tools for Fred's workshop lie on the kitchen table - Iris is going to help Billy wrap them to put under the tree. Billy is fretting about Fred. He does not like him to be out for long.

'Never mind, Billy. You and I can make our own fun right here,' says Iris and goes to put her arms round him. But thirteen-year-old Billy is not there with Iris in the big house waiting for Fred. He is five years' old, back on Southport beach where the man said the same thing.

'Never mind, Billy. You and I can make our own fun right here,' he said and then, Billy knows what comes next, he puts his arms round him. *And the bad thing happens.*

'No!' Billy snatches up the new Stanley knife from the kitchen table and when Fred comes home his wife is on the floor, unconscious, covered in blood; there is blood all over the wrapping paper, all over the kitchen, all over Billy. Billy sits in the corner on the floor, the knife still in his hand. He is crying but that does not stop Fred hitting him. 'I got the booby prize,' Billy is repeating under Fred's heavy breathing. He does not flinch.

Billy was isolated in secure accommodation for his own saftey. He often asked for Iris.

Monday 3rd December. 1989

Billy has been in custody for nearly a year. It takes time to muster the reports necessary for such a defence. No-one has any idea of Billy's motivation in attacking Iris. Counsel is uneasy. As a witness Billy is unpredictable and even after hours spent interviewing him with a translator, Godfrey will have trouble remaining faithful to his received dictum, 'Never ask your witness a question unless you already know what he will answer'. Billy's mind follows paths unknown to the analytical brain of his lawyer, Godfrey Dickens. There is no question to which he could stake his life on Billy's reply. He will be asking him as little as possible. He will do his best before the judge and *Blow me!* it turns out to be Johnnie Dalrymple. *Old chum from my devilling days. Stroke of luck!* Once in the robing room he has an exchange with Counsel for the Prosecution. Purbright is not a friend, learned or otherwise, but they were at school together. *Did Purbright have a Christian name?* If so it escapes Godfrey.

'Morning, Dickens Mi.' Charlie Dickens, two years older had been quite a character at school. Now he is Charles Dickens QC. Godfrey had never shaken off the 'Minor' soubriquet or the resentment. Purbright is not troubled by the greys of man's existence. He sticks to black and white. For him the case is sewn up. 'Like a dog, Godfrey. Done it once, can't trust it again. Often the person it loves most that it goes for. Not saying he's not affectionate, your young William what's-his-name, Walker, just lethal, that's all. I think you'll find Donald'll agree.'

'Donald?'

'Donald the Dewey, yes. Always sounds like a single malt to me, eh? Our master today as ever was.' Purbright, facing the mirror, straightens his wig and grimaces at his own unlovely face with an expression that does duty for a smile.

'I thought Johnnie was at the stand this morning.'

'Last minute change, old fruit. It's death-dealing-Donald. Keeps dogs of course, does Donald.' *Suck on that!* Purbright nods knowingly and swirls out of the room. Godfrey catches sight of himself looking forlorn. *Donald. Bugger.* Hopelessly Godfrey picks up his brief and follows Purbright into the arena. *Bring on the lions.* And there they are five men and true and seven women awaiting the best reality show in town. Someone will be voted off today. The reports from the forensic psychiatrist, the social worker, the adoption agency are piled neatly on counsel's lectern. Donald has his own copies and, as he said to Elspeth last night,

'None of them throw any light at all on what makes the luckless William tick. Complete mystery. Probably never know what was going on in his head. Just like old Egmont when he went for Giles.' Purbright would have been thrilled.

'What will happen to him, Donald?', asked Elspeth. 'Egmont had to be put down.' This without a trace of humour.

'Haven't heard all the evidence yet, but an RSU seems the most likely.'

'Criminally insane?'

'Strictly speaking we don't say that any more, Elspeth. But, yes. Between you and me, barking.' This time they both laughed, guiltily.

AT LAST BILLY stood before the court, frightened and bewildered. Iris had aged almost beyond recognition in the twelve months and her eldest son, Harry, assisted her into the court room when she was called. His mother's suffering has aged him too and the last traces of the warmhearted, careless young man he once was have vanished now. Iris Little takes the stand, a large, black woman with an intelligent face and a matching coat and felt hat. Iris gave her evidence and the court heard of the loving child Billy had been. She spoke quietly of the sudden and inexplicable violence he had unleashed upon her the previous December. The judge questioned her gently about her injuries - she moved very cautiously now - and her recuperation, the prognosis. None of it was good.

'Did the accused say anything as he came at you with the knife?'

'He said, he said..... the sea was out. He said, 'Why did we come when the sea was out?''

'What did you understand him to mean by this, Mrs. Little?'

'It was one of his stories, your Honour. He was always talking about the sea. Some trip they took him on when he was little, I think.' Iris pauses and collects herself. 'The thing is, your Honour, I knew Billy better than anyone. He was with us for seven years. Fred and I, we hardly noticed his you know, the way he speaks, in the end, I mean. We loved him. He was one of our family. But even so, Billy was a mystery to us. We had no idea what he thought, no way of telling how much he understood.' Resolutely she keeps her head turned away from the accused for she would dearly love to comfort Billy for what he has done. She knows how much he loves her, that what happened that night is as much a mystery to him as it is to her. But she has promised Harry and Fred. They have argued about it, but in the end she has promised. No more contact with Billy.

After the attack she had spent three months in hospital, mostly worrying about Fred who visited daily. Fred's health had suffered although it was only a very small heart attack, the doctor said. His harmless hours in the workshop were now lost to him. He had got rid of all his tools as soon as the ambulance had left. Harry had organised the clearing up in the kitchen but Fred never sat in there now. The days were long for Fred Little but Iris, lying in her hospital bed, opened her eyes at last on Christmas Day and he thanked God every day that she was still with him. They love each other very much.

Billy was called to speak but his most eloquent testimony came in the tears he shed when he saw Iris. When she left the stand, Iris passed close to Billy and a terrible noise came from him of pain and longing. Iris left the courtroom with dignity; she did not turn round. She automatically forgave him what he had done, but Billy's pain was too much for her and she had vowed that in future her duty was to Fred. She would no longer involve herself in Billy's fate except to tell the truth. Harry and Fred hated him, hated themselves, for what had happened to Iris.

'Mrs. Little,' said the judge, 'you have shown yourself to be a woman of uncommon generosity and courage and I would especially like to commend you for coming here today to help us decide what to do with William. Your evidence has been invaluable and we hope that you and your husband can now settle back into the peaceful family life that you deserve.' This with a nod at Harry.

'Please be kind to him, your Honour,' said Iris. Billy made a bellowing sound and twisted away from the warder in an attempt to bang his head against the nearby wall. Two male warders led him away.

STRANGELY KATE FOUND she thought more and more about the baby she had lost as she grew older. He had the right to trace her and at the back of her mind, she hoped and dreaded one day to get that letter, that phone call. What kind of man would he be, that little boy she had abandoned? Rob is back from Hull on Wednesday. Before then she can decide how to present herself to him and the boys. *Must do their rooms. What would they feel about a new baby?* With every day the presence inside her becomes more recognisably human. The baby and Billy weigh on her conscience when she speaks to Rob, as she does most days. She needs time to know how much she will share with him and how much will have been transformed by sleep and familiarity into 'the past', into a traumatic experience she can live with. Tonight Rob does not call, knowing she is out on duty. She leans against the aga, her warm-hearted friend, and sips a glass of red wine. The dresser winks at her with its French china and the warm tiles underfoot remind her how much she loves her home.

Sebastian has been the ideal son. He went straight to university from school, one that they had heard of. Now he has a lovely girlfriend and every prospect of a good job. Kate cannot believe she has such a straightforward son. As clever as his father, he is reading Law and means to go straight to The Bar. It gave her a warm feeling now when she thought of Seb, who was doing what Brian would have wanted. Max, meanwhile was the free spirit - perhaps only one twin has this licence. Right now he was travelling in North Africa, a second gap year.

'Will you speak to Dad, Mum?'

'A gap between what and what, exactly? 'asked Rob with irritation when Kate explained Max's plans. Max had already been travelling for a year.

'He'll come home ready to knuckle down, you'll see.' In reality, Kate rather hoped that Max never knuckled down. He was living her dream and she did not worry about him.

SHE HAS HIDDEN the leaflets from the surgery in a storage basket under the kitchen counter and averts her eyes as she passes them. *What is the point of having tests if you're not going to change your plans according to the results?* The sound of the river outside restores her peace of mind and soon she settles the dogs down, locks up and climbs the stairs. A truly rambling house, it is nevertheless a short step to Kate's bedroom with its tiny adjoining bathroom. Steps and corners betray the house's age and history. For a split second she admires this beautiful room and then sleep claims her and she exchanges the darkness of the bedroom for the all-encompassing peaceful blackness of her unconscious.

Sunday morning. 0712

It must be half an hour now since I woke. The phosphorescent fingers of the alarm clock are ambiguous. The December morning gives nothing away.

IN TOWN ANDY and Oliver are leaving the Samaritans' office. Oliver's first night duty has worn his face pale and hollow. Andy meanwhile is worried about Kate. *Too early to call her.*

I CAN NEVER make out this clock. Her hands automatically explore her belly. *Hello Baby. It's alright Baby.* Silently she tries the name 'Leila' on her tongue. *Just you and me tonight. A bit tired, that's all. I've got to find out about Billy. Can't sleep. Might as well do it now. Up we get. Find out what there is to know. Maybe we can go back to sleep then. Feet on the floor. Dressing gown on. I need to know I'm wrong, that Billy's not planning this for Wednesday. I need to be sure this only happens in his head, or in his past.* In her study Kate huddles at her desk, prodding the computer screen into life and dialling up. Broadband has yet to reach Kidbury where the river Test runs through her garden. Ritually she curses the delay and makes several errors as she types into the search engine what she is looking for. At length the results for Sefton Park are displayed.

"thieves will be caught red-handed if they continue to target allotments in Sefton Park' Merseyside Police"

"This crime alert covers Lark Lane from the entrance to Sefton Park to Aigburth Road' Business Crime Direct"

"'List of Centres for reporting hate crime in Sefton' sefton.gov.uk"

"'£1 million street lights boost for Liverpool' 24dash.com"

"'a gun crime conference at the Lace Centre, Sefton Park Drive' ahgtm.ac.uk"

No trace of any crime involving children in Sefton Park. Nothing in the nationals. What about the Echo? Kate used to read *The Liverpool Echo.* In her student house there had been an ongoing competition to find the cheapest article for sale in *The Echo* classifieds. The record stood at 45p. In this reverie, a pleasant break from Dorothy, she pauses over thoughts of Otty's Cafe where she had eaten every day with friends. There she had the joy of an English breakfast and large mugs of tea with the builders and bag ladies who formed its clientele. And, of course, they all smoked, stubbing out their B & H into the little foil rounds from jam tarts. A jar of pickled eggs stood on the counter. *Still never tasted a pickled egg.*

The archives are difficult to access but eventually she finds references to Sefton Park. *'Used for picnics', 'used for sponsored walks', 'used by the Brownies', gawd help us, 'a children's art exhibition'. How old is he? Anywhere between eighteen and fifty. How far back do I go? Thirty odd years? Twenty-five? Yes. No more than that. Let's try 'Dorothy' and 'Sefton Park'. What's this, "Dorothy Prescott"?*

"Dorothy Prescott (1890-1972) formerly of Allerton, Liverpool, responsible for

introducing to the park gardens an
anonymous species of Himalayan
clematis, now named in her honour."

Well, good old her.

"A vigorous plantswoman whose life's work
was to corral in her English garden as
many of the exotic growths as survived the
return journey from her far-flung
expeditions".

Well Billy, you're not having a picnic with her, are you? Oh shit, this is just what I didn't want. What am I doing. I cannot prove a negative. I cannot know for certain that nothing happened. Now I feel worse than before. I was sure I'd find something in the past. If this isn't your history, Billy, does it really lie in the near-future? I just can't believe you were making all that up. It cost you so much to tell me. I could feel your pain.

Sunday morning. 0803

Kate reads the clock on her computer. Sunlight filters through cloud touching the oak trees with colour. Kate remembers magic painting books where a brush and water alone could illuminate a whole page with different colours. She is thinking in hours now. On Wednesday morning Billy will attempt to consummate his love for Dorothy. *That must not happen.* I am the only person he has told and I am supposed to do nothing. She goes back to bed and plugs her iPod into her ears so that Alan Bennet reading 'Winnie The Pooh' can fill her head as she sleeps. *Keep Billy out. And my mother.*

Sunday morning. 1008

THE TELEVISION NEWS is on again. *'Police looking for Polly and Dorothy Brown have found the body of a child in Sefton Park'*. The announcer smooths her perfect hair with a heavily jewelled hand and morphs into Kate's mother. *'Polly and Dorothy have not been seen since they left for school yesterday morning. Their parents have told the police that someone heard Dorothy crying for help but did nothing, told no-one'.* Kate wakes up clutching her precious stomach, tears sticky in her eyes. She thought morning sickness had passed. *Do nothing.* Pressing her forehead to the cold tiles in the loo, she sees behind her tired eyelids the newly bereaved parents.

THEY ARE ONCE again removed from the public arena, returned to their home. She hears fragments of dialogue. *"Only one body." "Not our girls then." "Listen love, that body could have been there years."* They cleave to each other and to the pathologist's cautious words, his refusal to draw the inevitable conclusion. But Pauline in the kitchen no longer chats. As soon as there are bodies she must distance herself from the suffering of parents who become suspects. She is required to report on them; she cannot afford to identify with them. With practice her withdrawal, her distance, is masked as respect. The tragedy develops as surely as a glass of water breaks on a stone floor. The shards of glass, the pools of water foreshadowing pools of blood, 'Put your shoes on!' They exist as soon as the elbow catches the tumbler.

FIVE

KATE PASSES HER Sunday with the dogs and the papers in front of the fire. Above the snoring of the dogs and the crackle of the fire, Kate's mobile rings. *That'll be Andy......or Rob.* It is Andy and she can hear in his voice the natural chivalry of his generation. Again her father is with her. Andy is anxious not to be chauvinistic, always updating his vocabulary and rooting out newly inappropriate assumptions which spring like bindweed in a rose garden. This was something her father did not live long enough to attempt. It was hard for Kate to imagine him having had any truck with it actually. 'Never apologise, Kate. Never explain'. His advice had seemed deliberately contentious when she was twenty; recently it had begun to sound like common sense. Andy, meanwhile, is solicitous but not patronising with the 'lady Sams', 'women' as he has now learned to call them. To him the word sounds coarse and ungracious but they seem to like it. Kate argues briefly and without any hope of success about what they should do. *About Billy.*

'Are you having trouble with our policy, Kate? Not interfering, total confidentiality? I know it seems hard, but how can we do anything without betraying your caller's confidence?'

'But Andy, he could end up in prison for something and he has no idea how serious it is what he is going to do. This isn't just about the little girl. This is about the caller!'

'What about all our other callers, Kate? If we make exceptions we will lose our credibility. We will be just one more interfering agency and our callers will have no-one they can trust.'

'Andy, I don't expect to do anything myself. I know my work stops with my call. But surely you can tell me that someone senior will deal with this? Surely someone will be calling the police in Liverpool and doing what they can? I don't need to know any details, just tell me something will be done, that Billy will be protected from himself and Dorothy from him. That'll be enough for me.'

But Andy was adamant. He could give her no such assurance. It was against policy. *I have to tell you now - Chamberlain's endlessly broadcast voice. War followed swiftly.* Later, Deputy Director Gretel calls. She has been alerted by Andy; dissidence in the ranks. She wants to support Kate, she says. *Support me to do nothing.* Kate assents but tells Gretel that she cannot agree with the policy, that she is acting against her own moral instinct. A short, wet walk with the dogs punctuates the afternoon but still Kate is involved in her internal drama.

'IT'S ME. I'M just calling to say I'm on my way.' Just a few weeks ago Kate had driven up to Harrogate to see her mother. This was a birthday visit for Marilyn and Kate is apprehensive as ever. *I'll take her out to lunch. Give her a chance to dress up a bit - I know how she likes that. Let me show you the things I've bought, that's what she always says as soon as I've had the obligatory cup of coffee. It used to be so easy when the boys were little.* In those days, she never ran out of things to talk to Marilyn about and although Granny had opinions about discipline, she was a huge fan of her grandsons. Marilyn would cook them the same apple crumble and cottage pie that she had fed Kate as a child. This was the way she knew to show and to receive love.

Now when Kate pulls in to the tidy driveway, she is holding herself braced against the remarks that will come.

'You won't approve, but I've bought a new dining table,' Marilyn greets her.
Kate, who hates the way her childhood home has been stripped of it contents and 'improved' over the years, for once sees an old lady desperate for Kate to accept her.

'Well, you'd better show me!' she replies brightly and Marilyn peers at her warily over her glasses as if uncertain how to respond. The visit was not without its sticky patches, but for Kate there was a softening which made it less painful than usual. Perhaps her work with Sue was helping. Marilyn was full of praise for Kate 'driving all that way' and thanked her repeatedly for coming.

'Ring me when you get home.' *Thank God that's over.*

SHE'LL BE HERE soon. Everything's ready. I laid the table the day before yesterday and everything's ready. Milk in the jug for her coffee - she has to have coffee, but it won't do for me. Serviettes on the table - napkins, Mummy! What will she think of this skirt? Shall I change? I've tried wearing the things she likes but it doesn't feel like me. They're too good for me. It's not the money, it's... Trouble is I can hear our Mum. "Who do you think you are, Marilyn, going out like that? Princess Margaret? What do you look like? Are you from round here or are we not good enough for you? That's what they all felt when I met Brian. 'We're not good enough for you'. Even Bessy.

She'll come in that big car - I hope the neighbours don't see. I'll never get used to having a daughter called Kate, never crossed my mind to call her Kate. I wish I'd been different, more what she wanted. Bound to raise her eyebrows when she sees what I'm wearing. 'What happened to that nice Jaeger outfit we bought? What are you wearing that old thing for? I thought I'd take you out to lunch, anyway. So go on, dress up a bit.' I don't want to go out to lunch. I want to use the new dining table. It's all ready here. She'll smile in that superior way and say 'Oh, I might have known you'd have it all ready. What's wrong with a bit of spontaneity, Mother?'

She throws meals together, you see. Brilliant too, I've seen them. I've eaten them. Open her fridge and there's nothing in it, but ten minutes later we're all sitting down to what she calls an Italian lunch, dishes of this, plates of that - she thinks nothing of the washing up. I've stopped offering to do a few potatoes. That's what we did at home - mid-morning one of us girls would do a few potatoes, ready for dinner. They always have bread or pasta or something. Anyway, if I offer to help she puts on that thinking face and looks into the distance. Then she smiles at me and says 'I don't really know what we're having yet'. Don't know what we're having yet! Can you imagine? It could be six o'clock. Her children have eaten things I can't spell. Max and Sebastian. My grandsons. Those lovely boys. I did love having them when they were little. They used to stay with me and I loved reading to them. Now they're like her. They make me feel I know nothing, I've been nowhere. I've had my whole life, nearly and they know more than me already. I'm not a very nice person, am I? Fancy being jealous of my own grandchildren. No, Marilyn, you're not all you pretend to be by a long chalk. She'll be here soon. Shall I change the skirt? Shall I? Whatever I do it'll be wrong. They go through into the dining room. To Kate's surprise there were hundreds of cards and some presents on the mantelpiece.

'Gosh, Mummy, you've done awfully well.' *She's pleased with me.*

'Yes, I have, haven't I? They're all from my friends at church, of course. Don't know how they knew. Perhaps the Vicar put them all on notice. I've made a list of them all and who they're from.'

'To write your thank you letters?'

'No, it's my birthday diary. I like to have a record of the day. What I ate, who came, what presents I got.'

'Oh, I see.' Kate always forgets that her mother still yearns to be a wanted child.

Sunday evening. 1800

KATE HAS SPENT an hour at her computer watching videos of foetal development on YouTube. She clicks on the thumbnail and conception is shown. It looks as she knew it would like the moon landings of her childhood. She closes the screen and begins to search for a site selling Spring seeds - she is too late to plant bulbs. She registers for a catalogue. Her internal life is returning to something approaching normal. There is plenty to do towards

Christmas and her anxiety has died down. She has returned to her immediate concern - the baby. *How to tell Rob?* She and the baby have lain together in the double bed night after night and that tiny person is as real to her as the rest of her family. She is into Month Two - 'your baby will be approximately one half to three quarters of an inch long and weigh about one to two grams by the end of this month' reads Kate. *Fingers, toes, the heart-beat all happen in the next four weeks. Unbelieveable. A huge energy arises - I must protect this child at all costs.*

KATE HAS AN hour's nap on the sofa and a long chat with Rob. She talks to him about inconsequential things, presents, social engagements. *I must make him see how precious this life is. The last we shall create.*

He is full of the place he is staying, the weather, the journey and how he misses her. At least, that is what he is full of when he speaks to her. She often feels she does not exist for him when he is away and busy. A familiar sadness clutches at her heart. For her, on the other hand, his absence ensures he is never out of her thoughts. They share a private joke about one of Rob's employees and chat about the children. No longer children. It is easy for Kate not to tell him anything she does not want to; she describes her relaxing day inside, the dogs' antics and accepts his gentle concern for her health. *If only he knew...*

'Two nights running, Katie. Must you? Don't overdo it.' It is dark again. But the truth is that he likes her busy so that he can be more so. She wants him there. After they have said goodbye there is the pull and ache of sadness within, soon anaesthetised by folding herself and her child into the safety of the future. *He will be home soon.* Then she can let go, decide what to do.

Time to start getting ready. Not really a night duty, only eight to eleven. She needs to leave at seven fifteen to get there in time for the ten minute hand-over period and now begins to clear up the kitchen and make a sweet cup of tea keeping one eye on the television and the dogs oblivious on the rug. Keeper and Bracken are nine and three. It had taken very little persuasion by the twins for them to get a dog when they moved to the Mill House. Keeper came first, black and beautiful with long legs and huge paws and a noble head. Completely brainless. Three years later, ' He's lonely, Mummy!', came Bracken. A different kind of dog altogether. Short-legged, intelligent and wilful. Bracken had no noble air but more of a slouch. Frank Sinatra to Keeper's Cary Grant. Even now when they came home Seb and Max roll on the rug with these wonderful, sloppy creatures and complain bitterly afterwards about the distinctive labrador smell. *Eau de l'abrador.*

Right now the dogs keep their heads down. They know full well that Kate is on her way out. If they cannot read her thoughts, they can certainly sense her energy patterns. Keeper lifts one ear, opens one eye and exchanges a glance with Bracken. Silently they agree. *Let's pretend it's not happening. Cold night. Better off in here.* Doesn't work of course. Kate is standing by the back door minutes later and both dogs instinctively leap to their feet and file outside. They stand on the lawn under the stars looking at each other accusingly. *Another fine mess you got me into.*

Sunday evening. 1920

BILLY STIRS IN his sleep. It is too bright in here. He is back in the narrow bed with the sides on that he remembers of old. Always daylight. If he shouts, voices shout back at him and he knows he's been bad again. He closes his eyes and sees again the Autumn leaves, the little blond head. He can almost taste the cake, sweet in his mouth. But no. There is the taste of blood, salt and metal on his lips. He cries in his sleep. He has bitten his tongue. It is nearly time. Billy has had his birthday on a Wednesday ever since he can remember.

Sunday evening. 1930

I HATE THE dual carriageway in the dark. Headlights blinding on the bends. My eyes are tired. Parking is no problem at this time, though. Swing the VW easily into that space outside the front door. Leave my phone in the car. Can't use it in there anyway. Lock the car. Samaritans. Front door. Stab the code into the keypad. One set of doors; two; and finally the door to the ops' room. Two unknown heads are bowed low over their calls and Melanie, the third person there, looks up from the admin desk as I enter. She's on with me then.The silent greeting. 'Hi Melanie'. *I'm glad it's Mel.* Two Sams work each shift and they must overlap their duties by ten minutes to pass on information about ongoing situations. This evening Pat and Shirley are going off duty; Mel and Kate are coming on.

Melanie, mid-fifties, tall, elegant, androgynous. She's had her hair cut. Blond, dark grey eyes, lovely face.Linen clothes in neutral colours, heavy jewellery she buys herself. Looks Scandinavian but actually American. Very little accent but that kind of polish they have. Perfect teeth. Glossy. Mel can be really funny, full of stories, often at her own expense. Frank left some years ago and took up with a less successful lady. She and Kate had grown close while this was happening. *Melanie at my dinner table. Rob too wrapped up in her to notice what he's eating, or the other guests, or that I am clearing the table again. Alone. Did she encourage him? Ridiculous to be jealous of Mel but there it is. Rob has rather a thing for older women. Remember Davina.* Kate has lunch with Mel now and again but only about half as often as they talk about it. Right now Mel jumps up when she sees Kate come in. *She's looking concerned, getting up and taking me outside into the corridor to ask me 'if I am alright after last night'. Do I still want to go ahead with my duty? I feel a flare of anger in my stomach. What the fuck? What's it got to do with her?*

'News travels fast, doesn't it? '

'Yes, Kate. We call that support, remember?' says Mel reproachfully. Kate does not realise she has spoken aloud. Mel is crossing her long legs and leaning back in her chair to look at her speculatively. Kate hides her anger with a deliberately rueful smile as if she were revealing something she would rather conceal. In reality she plays down the call from Billy.

'Hey look, that call has been preying on my mind but to be honest, Mel, I am better here and busy rather than unoccupied at home. Rob's away.' She does not want Mel to know what she feels.

Sunday evening 2010

'Have you made enquiries about Billy?' Kate has Gretel on the phone.

'I am afraid Liverpool have never heard of him. '

'Not a regular caller then?'

'I guess not.' They both know what that means. He's new. He's genuine.

'Kate, are you OK?'

'Yes, I'm fine. Honestly. Absolutely.'

'Will you call me tomorrow morning? Kate? '

'Yes.' *No. If his story is a fantasy, wishful thinking that he just wants to talk about, he would have done it before. Someone would have heard this story before. Men like that are regular callers. Those men are known to us, known to the organisation. Why don't we know Billy?* Pat is on the office phone reporting to Gretel about the shift he is just leaving.

'Yeah, I spoke to someone who wanted to fantasise about other men. Yeah, I didn't ask him the right questions and he went silent. So I said, 'What are you hoping to get out of your call to us this evening' and he said 'A wank'! He hung up.'

Laughter. A small space with two people coming in and two leaving. Limited coat hooks, bags to put down, parking permits to hand in, the log book to sign. Bit of a muddle for a while. Soon Shirley also finishes her call with relief and prepares to go home. Her vacated 'phone rings and Melanie takes the call.

'Samaritans. Can I help you? ' While Mel listens and occasionally speaks into the receiver, jotting down a few notes which she will later shred before leaving the building, Kate recapitulates in her head - a dry run for explaining to Mel, for getting Mel on her side. She can already hear the special pleading in her voice. *So. Billy. Is this a crime committed long ago? Now you need absolution? Could easily be. If so it's a crime which went undetected or unreported in Liverpool at the time. Even so, why is there no record of a Dorothy going missing? And what of the other child?* In her mind Kate has christened her Polly and made her Dorothy's elder sister. *Two children disappear together and no bodies are ever found, so no crime report. Surely it would make the local paper at least. Have I missed the year? How can I find out how old he is? Nothing in the newspaper indexes for the last thirty years. I would have thought it was a park just crying out for an assault, but there you go. Which leaves?* The possibility that the story is true.

BILLY HAS FORGOTTEN how old he is. He only knows that his birthday is one Wednesday in December and that he misses Iris and long-ago Gladys and that the missing is something to do with his birthday. The little girls in Sefton Park were a long time ago now. No-one will let him talk about them.

MEL IS OFF the phone and is updating herself with the Message Book. Here Sams communicate with each other about fund-raising events, house-keeping issues, and above all the rota. Offers to swap shifts and desperate pleas from the rota secretaries to fill duties in the coming days. Less urgent messages also find expression here. 'Can we have more black biros please?' 'Could people please NOT put ginger nuts in the biscuit tin as they flavour ALL the biscuits and some of us don't like ginger!' Sometimes Kate reads the Message Book just for laughs. Sounds like Mel has found something now.

'Have you seen this? Someone has written here ...' But the phone interrupts again with its permitted three rings and Kate moves to answer making a note of the time as she does so to log later. *Twenty o five.*

'Samaritans. Can I help you?' And another soul disrobes itself before Kate's prurient mind's eye. *God, I really don't want to do this tonight. Why do I feel this way? Whatever I do there is a risk of exploiting the caller.* The caller's name is Sue. *OK. Here we go. Well she's not drunk, nor obviously disturbed and yet... There is something about her story... Amazing,* thinks Kate, *how the paranoid, the depressed and the frankly barking mad reveal their condition so slowly and yet inevitably in such inconsequential ways. Our lives are full of tragedy, most of which never happens. Who said that?*

Each conversation so fragile. Each communication inevitably distorted by the listener. It is of course the clinically sane who sound mad. They shout and rave, pushed at last beyond their limits by the death of a child, the affair, divorce, drug problems, debt. They threaten self-harm, revenge and violence, most of which does not transpire. The hopelessly deranged are different. Some struggle to have their own experience through a fog of medication, and resent it. For others, medication might provide relief, but it has not been offered yet. They have not yet set their foot to the treadmill of waiting lists, psychiatrists, assessment. The labyrinthine mental health system is like a mirror of the dazed patient's mind.

It takes a while before people notice Sue's very particular reality - and when they do they back off and she is left, again, angry and bewildered. She remembers without rancour the small, dark, Winter bedroom her mother sent her to for punishment, the mother against whom she will permit no word of censure. All her anger is for people in the present who challenge her in any way.

'Well, I'd been naughty, hadn't I? Never did me a bit of harm.' Sue loved her cold, witholding mother with a passion. 'If only parents today weren't frightened of a bit of discipline, a good smack never hurt anyone! Look at me!' Kate is chilled inside listening to Sue. And so on. The voice runs in her head night and day. It was always Winter in that small bedroom, unheated still in 1962. Despite her large, warm house, she seems to live there now in that bedroom. No room in there for a man, for children. Hardly any room for Sue. Friends are allowed as far as the door. Kate can picture her house, its stained glass still intact above the front door, the well-washed tiles in the entrance hall; her clothes, good but not extravagant and with little touches of femininity - her mother's brooch, the surprising beads from the Cathedral gift shop. Sue owns more occasional scarves than there are occasions in her life. A look skillfully and unconsciously put together to indicate decent, lower middle class, female but unavailable. We all have our uniforms. Her body is an unknown continent to her. It is kept clean and fed as once the infant Sue was, but pleasure, exploration, the excitement of personal contact, these things were not deemed necessary, in fact they were frowned upon. Now, to Sue, they feel like sin. Letting go of the rules her mother taught her would mean letting go of her mother and she feels her world rock at the very thought. Instead she judges the outside world which breaks these rules very harshly. The word 'disgusting' is often on her lips.

Once upon a time she thought she was looking for a husband but, well-trained by her mother who brooked no competition, she presents herself scrupulously to the world as single and destined to remain so. She might as well have a printed label across her well-developed chest. She has watched as less attractive girls paired off and produced children, as they disappeared into an intricate web of family commitments and now, well, she's not sure that would have suited her after all. They had had to compromise, most of them.

So why is she calling? Why does she imagine she is calling. Kate is about to find out.

'I can't find them, I've looked everywhere.'

'So, you've been through all the possibilities?'

'I've looked everywhere and now I'm wondering if somebody's taken them.'

'Is that possible?'

'Well no-one's been in the house that I know of. But I don't like to think of it, someone coming in and taking them.'

'Have you let anyone in?'

'Only the man who delivered something. Do you think it was him? I suppose it could've been him.'

'Well, we don't know. Did he come into the house?' Sue has lost some ear plugs. She fears they may have been stolen. At first Kate thinks there must be a misunderstanding, but no. A small box of ear-plugs. *Boots'* own. 'No, I just signed the thing while he stood on the step.'

'So no-one's been in the house?'

'Only my friend. My friend came round to help me look for them. She wouldn't take them, I know she wouldn't. I mean she's not a close friend but she wouldn't take them.'

'And you last saw them where?'

'When I unpacked. They were in my case and I put them on the hall table. I unpacked in the hall, you see.'

'Uhuh...'

'Only I got back late at night. I was tired.' The note of self-justification is unprovoked by anything Kate has said. It is a tone learned long ago in response to endless, unwarranted criticism. A tired, six-year-old wipes her dirty hands on her dress and off she goes again to the purdah of that cold room. The sting of her mother's palm on her calves, of her words in her ears. In her head the protest she cannot voice. 'I was tired'. This is now the only conversation Sue can have whether she is buying a newspaper or wishing you Happy Birthday - the aching need to defend herself is constant and by some metaphysical imperative she hears you attack her whatever you say. She has few friends. *Tread very carefully.* 'Mmmm? You were tired....'

'I was tired so that's why I didn't unpack until next morning.'

'Did you go somewhere nice?'

I don't know about nice. I went to India. That's why I bought the ear plugs. For the plane.' Kate reels. Her prejudices had placed Sue safely in mainland Europe and probably no further than Wales. 'Wow, that's quite a holiday.'

'Yes. It was. It wasn't what you'd call a relaxez-vous kind of holiday though. It was all go. I had a struggle really, keeping up and then there was my tummy. Do you know you can't get Milk of Magnesia out there. Funny, isn't it? You'd think they'd need it there.' Kate backtracks. A passage to India had presented for Sue the same kaleidoscope of suffering as a day trip to Bournemouth. Foreign things waiting to get her. A sinking sense of being in the wrong. A growing hatred of the other tourists who are having a good time.

'It sounds quite a difficult time...'

'It was.' Sue's voice does not soften when sympathy is forthcoming. She does not respond to subtle variations of tone or body language. Her personality renders her experience of the outside world dull and repetitive, the same as her inside world. 'You'd had a long flight.'

'Yes. I was disoriented and what-not and what-not. But I saw them when I unpacked next day. I shouldn't have left the case in the hall, should I? Not overnight? They wouldn't have disappeared if I'd taken it upstairs.'

'I expect you were too tired to do that then.'

'Yes, but now I can't find them and it's driving me up the garden path. I mean they were only cheapy little items. But they were mine. My own personal business. I don't want people interfering in my own personal business.' Sue has lost the earplugs she bought for the plane journey, now over. She says she is not suicidal but that she has spent two days constantly looking for them, has had someone to help her look for an afternoon and now she is wondering if she should knock on her neighbours' door and see if they have them. This is a major event for Sue and this is the second time she has called to talk about it. Earlier she spoke to another branch. For Kate it is torture. The conversation can have no end since Sue can neither find her ear plugs nor is she interested in discussing why this might be affecting her so deeply.

What, in God's name, do these earplugs represent? 'Have you thought...? I mean, is it just the ear plugs? Is there something else worrying you?' *Your life, for example? Your sanity?* 'What do you mean?' *Blank mystification. OK. No more we can do.*

Kate makes a decision. They are half an hour into this conversation and whatever the earplugs represent for Sue, was lost long ago : the space to be herself, perhaps, the freedom not to be constantly improved, overruled and banished. The possibility of intimacy. The feeling that 'people' have always been 'interfering' is like the air she breathes. A world full of opportunities, full of pleasure, contact, fulfilment is not Sue's world. All that can be done in this 'phone call is to soothe her and keep her company as she finds a way to move on out of this corner of the maze. But the maze with its stale air is all there is. It is her natural habitat. Outside, the oxygen of real life would kill her.

'Of course not. Maybe you could just buy some more? If they weren't um, expensive?' *She does not understand.* 'That's not the point. I need to know where they are.' *She's mad.* 'Yes, I can see that. Have you thought you might have put them in a safe place. Perhaps you won't ever find them and it will only make you unhappy to keep on wondering.' 'That's what my friend said.' 'Well I think she's right.' *Omigod.*

Kate logs the call. A jar of pens stands by each telephone so that a record is made. At the end of the shift loose papers are shredded for reasons of confidentiality. The log book alone remains. *Start time 2005. Length of call 42 minutes. Caller female, Age unknown. No suicidal feelings.* Brief description. Kate writes, *'single lady worried about ear plugs she has lost'* and turns to Mel.

'You couldn't make them up could you? Did you hear all that?'

'Poor old soul. I thought you were very nice to her though.'

'I wanted to scream.'

'There's so many of them aren't there, living out there on their own?'

'No wonder,' mutters Kate. *I am really not in the mood for Mel to be nice.*

'What about you? Are you OK?'

'Yeah, I'm fine. Just sometimes you go through a whole call not only feeling you're not getting anywhere but also feeling like a really horrible person. Some people are just so hard to sympathise with.'

'You did fine, God, you're still recovering from last night. Now stop worrying about her and tell me about Billy.'

Sunday evening. 2050

Mel puts down the Caller Care News folder and settles herself down with her cold cup of tea. Kate can at last run through the possibilities that have been haunting her. She respects Mel. *She has a good brain. I'd like to know what she thinks.* She tells Mel the story, the phone call, how she has searched the net to check the past and found nothing and how the pressure of Billy's imminent birthday and his plans for celebrating it are dominating her thoughts. Mel listens quietly. A therapist and experienced Sam, she is slow to comment and when she does it is not the reponse Kate hoped for.

'You know you have to let this go, don't you?'

'But Mel I...'

'This will only make you unhappy,' Kate's protests dry upon her lips. It is her turn to listen and she knows it. *Fuck! Why did I tell her?* Kate is the more annoyed since Mel is obviously concerned for her. 'Look, once in a while, a call like this comes.' *Well thank you ma'am. May I take notes?* 'It is the call you will always remember. You were there for him, for Billy, yesterday and no-one could have done better than you did. You really heard him. He really opened up to you. That's the absolute best we can do. The rest is not for us. We are the only ear Billy and people like Billy have. The others, the little girls have their parents, teachers, the police, the rest of society. Billy has no-one. You betray him and he has no-one.' Mel leans back in her chair and crosses her long legs. *Sexy black boots beneath the wrap around skirt.*

'I know, but...' Kate's voice peters out. Mel has no axe to grind.

'Imagine, Kate. No-one ever hears Billy, no-one can bear to wait whilst he gets the words out, but you did wait. You may never know what the truth is, the historical truth, the truth that gets in the newspapers. That's not the point. You heard his truth as it was at that moment when he was telling you. You can't do any more.' A pause. Kate looks at the carpet.

'The thing is, Mel, it is as much for Billy that I want to intervene. Suppose this is just a fantasy he has lived with for years, but now he might act. His life will be over. No-one will ever understand why he did it. Just another monster for the public to hate. We could help. Maybe.'

'How? How could we help without betraying your caller?'

'I don't know. I assumed that I would not have to think about it.'

'You don't.'

'I *mean*, I assumed that in a case like this, a case where something terrible could be prevented, the powers that be would get in touch with the police, warn them, tip them off, whatever.' Mel makes a helpless gesture. 'A policeman walking through that park would scare Billy off and if he gets past his birthday I don't think he will try again.'

'Do you know they are not getting in touch? Has anybody said anything?'

'Yes, I got the big lecture from Andy last night about non-intervention. He hoped that Liverpool would know him and that I could stop worrying if he was a regular caller with the same story each time.' Mel gulps down the last of her cold tea as she says,

'But they don't?'

'No. Then I've had Griselda on the phone several times making sure I am not going to do anything and making it clear that no-one else is either. 'Not Samaritan policy'.' Kate sighs deeply. 'It's not right, Mel. What harm would it do to call the Liverpool police? Anonymously even? Two children at risk has to be worth an hour of police time, doesn't it?'

'No-one can stop you, Kate, but I don't recommend it.'

'No.' Mel purses her lips and waits a minute before making a new start.

'But this isn't just about Billy, is it? This is a problem with authority, isn't it?' Mel acknowledges Kate's wilful smile with a slight tilt of her head. 'You can't just accept the rules when you feel it's right and then break them when you don't. The Samaritans would fall to pieces if everyone did that. Callers wouldn't know where they were.'

'Yes, I know all that. I just never thought it would feel so wrong. I...' Her impatience is getting the better of Kate now but the telephone rings and Mel leaps up, glad to avoid hearing more. *You can't reevaluate the rules you signed up for just because once in a lifetime you get a difficult call. Can you?* Mel does not say this but Kate hears it anyway and hostility comes to the surface. *She should stick to life-coaching,* she thinks nastily, forgetting that Mel has given her a proper hearing. Suddenly she remembers that dinner as if it were yesterday! Mel gazing at Rob as if he were the Second Coming while Kate is clearing the table again. Suddenly there is nothing Kate likes about her at all.

Mel's call is a mental health patient. *Do the CPNs know how often they ring? Like, all the time.* Community psychiatric nurses are not available at night, or weekends as Samaritans well know. *Does it help, our listening? Does it make any difference whether we really open ourselves to the caller giving every ounce of ourselves for however long it takes? Trying to piece together their story from the endless repetition, trying to find out what it's like to be them tonight? Seems like it wouldn't make any difference if you were reading a book, they just talk right through you anyway.* Kate stops, realising that she is mentally undermining the whole Samaritan ethos in order to feel better about the conflict regarding Billy.

Sunday evening. 2123

THE OTHER PHONE rings and Kate leaves her thoughts and the email she was ostensibly reading.

'Samaritans. Can I help you?' It is Billy. Through silence Kate discerns the tiny, internal noises of a man unable to speak. *I am sure it is Billy.* As the caller hangs up there is the sound of someone whose body is out of control.

This is a person for whom fine motor control has been lost. *Or never emerged.* He does not hang up with one finger; he cuts off the call with his whole body. There is the clumsiness of the receiver going down in a world where the gap between intention and outcome is unavoidably large. Imagine a sober life with all the delicacy and expertise, all the self-judgments of a drunk. What kind of pain is that?

Sunday evening. 2124

'The other person has hung up. The other person...' The recorded voice fills in the void. *Damn. I've lost him. The receiver is heavy in my hand, the print on the wall a few inches away illegible, meaningless. Concepts are driven out of my head by the insistent sensations in my body, the heaviness of my heart, the lead in my feet where they connect with the floor, a frozen energy vibrating in my arms. I kind of knew I would get him again. This isn't over for either of us yet.* Mel's voice reaches Kate in this timeless moment and she swivels her chair and arranges her face for her. Mel has finished her own call.

'Kate? That was David, you know, the one who used to be an athlete?' Of a sudden, Kate's feelings about Mel have swung back again. *OK, Rob may fancy her, but that's not her fault. She's a good sort, a genuine friend when I need one. I can trust her. Whatever was all that about before?* Kate is horrified at how her moods swing to and fro. *Is this what being pregnant is like?*

'How was he?'

'Oh, you know. He's missed some of his medication and then taken too much at once to make up. He was quite hard to understand. Such a sweet guy. Always so grateful, so apologetic.' Mel is bending over the log. 'Was yours a snap? Shall I log it for you? Kate, wake up!' *Out of a buried place I say 'yes'.* Is there a delay before she says 'yes'? A split second where the consequences of choosing this path are foreseen, measured and accepted? Or is it really without thinking as she will claim? This is where her lonely journey begins that is to end in a traffic jam on the A34. *Well it was a snap, wasn't it? I'm guessing it was Billy and I could be wrong. No-one spoke. It was a snap.*

'Kate, are you OK? You shouldn't have come in today, you know.' Out of her natural honesty, some long-ago-learned need for absolution, a desire arises in Kate to confide. She is going to tell Mel that she cannot comply, that she must do something about Billy. She has heard all the reasons why not and her instinct is still to intervene, to prevent if possible, a tragedy which will wreck a dozen lives. *He will call again and when he does... When he does... what?* But just as she is about to open up to Mel, somewhere between her heart and her mouth, there is a twist or turn, unknown perhaps to Kate herself and when she speaks it is to offer up a different secret. She does confide in Mel but not about Billy, not about the 'snap'. She fobs off her instinct for honesty with a different truth as you might throw your picnic to a marauding dog in a foreign country. She makes an acceptable sacrifice to protect something else, in this case, something darker. She explains away her strange mood, and now she is not sure as she talks whether it is indeed her pregnancy that is responsible for her feelings after all. Mel's honest face makes Kate feel innocent. *If people believe you, are you telling the truth? I mean, I haven't done anything. It probably wasn't even him. That's why callers get angry when you do not believe them.* Untruths lie like yesterday's fish in the rubbish bin; the stench is uncontainable. Kate prepares to leave the straight and narrow at the very next fork in the path. *Here it comes.*

Sunday evening. 2130

'The thing is, Mel, I'm pregnant.' In her head the echoes of the past. *The thing is, Dad, I'm pregnant. The thing is, Rob, I'm pregnant.*

'Oh, Kate! Gosh! ' *The American twang in the English idiom.* Now it is Mel's turn to control her features, choosing a non-committal expression of surprise, ready to incorporate with a crinkling of her eyes, celebration or sympathy on cue. *She must be forty-five, her twins are... eighteen? nineteen? university anyway.* Deliberately Mel walks over and takes the two phones off the hook. Kate open her mouth to protest and then doesn't.

'How do you feel?' A stock-in-trade of the Samaritan, the question with a thousand meanings offers Kate a range of possible responses. They both laugh; they both sober up quickly.

'I'm not sure, to be honest. I mean I feel tired and I have been sick but that is passing now.' Much remains unsaid but audible.

'Mmm, how long...?' *A question so open you could fall into it. A crevasse.*

'I found out for definite a week ago, just after Rob went away. Before that I didn't know what was wrong with me. I just felt weird.' A relief for Mel as she can adjust her face into the familiar pattern of compassion. Women know profoundly how their bodies call the shots and how their lives are often on hold, waiting for things to get clearer. Am I pregnant? Hiding the packets with their tell-tale phials and testing strips first from mother, then the lover, the boss, the husband. Trying to pee into things at school, in the office loo. The heart-in-mouth breathlessness looking for that blue line, pink line, whatever. Willing it to appear. Willing it not to. Part of you always hoping to see it and part of you alive with dread. The relief. I'm pregnant! I'm not pregnant! Or the despair. The blood, the tears. All this is in Mel's face now. Women together.

As she speaks Billy fades into the background and the urgency of telling Rob about the baby really does come to the fore.

'Does he know?'

'Not yet.' *So there it is. She has not told him.* Kate can see judgment in Mel's face. The silent protest within. *I haven't told anyone! He's been away!*

'Ah. So how pregnant are you? Do you know?'

'About four weeks is my guess.'

'And when does Rob get back?'

'Another week, ten days. He's doing a round trip. 'Oop North." Kate does the joke accent. 'He's seeing all the clients and potential clients who are too far away to visit on an everyday basis.' There is a pause while they both consider all the other things Rob could be doing over a two-week spree in the local Malmaison hotel. Then Mel ponders why Kate has not told Rob about the baby.This can only mean one of two things. She wants the baby and thinks he won't or she does not want the baby and thinks he will. No, there is a third thing. She has not decided yet. And she wants to decide without him. All of these things are difficult. All involve betrayal. Mel feels for her. She never did have children with Frank. *There were some near-misses though. And the pain still lingers. Too late now.*

Meanwhile Kate is also wondering whom will she betray? *Rob? The baby? Billy?* 'It's complicated,' she tells Mel. *So she has not decided. It is the third type of betrayal.* 'I was shocked when I found out. I did a test, you know and then I went to the doctor and he confirmed it. I know it's mad but it was impossible not to be happy. I just came away on cloud nine. I know I'm stupid.'

'But?' *Does she know this hurts me to talk about?*

'But when I got home I read the stuff the doctor had given me, information, leaflets, you know and it was all about birth defects, all the different deadlines, amniocentesis, scans, blood tests. Loads of stuff. I couldn't believe what they've thought of since I had the twins. You'd think I had some life-threatening condition, not just a baby.'

'Because of your age?'

'Yeah, because of my age. He tried to warn me in the surgery - he said the risk was one in thirty of Downes Syndrome at my age, but I wasn't really listening. I never had to go through this before, now there's a lot of pressure. Now it feels like I have to spend most of my pregnancy wondering whether to bond with this baby or whether a test result will suddenly pop up and someone in a white coat will recommend we get rid of it. As if it were a cold or something. Something inconvenient. You know they abort babies now who will need minor surgery? Really easily corrected things like a club foot or a hare lip. And I know what Rob would say.' Kate feels a brief pang for the baby she gave up all those years ago. *Not aborted but lost all the same.*

'So you think you're about four weeks?'

'Yes, I reckon so. You know I could so easily wake up not pregnant in the next few weeks - apparently that's even more likely to happen over forty, spontaneous miscarriage - it just doesn't seem worth facing a row with Rob.'

'Why a row?'

Inside her floats a small creature whose eyes cannot open for another six months, who cannot yet hear ('Month Five. Baby may be able to hear you now'); yet she feels all her mother's fear and confusion as if it were her own. Her entire physical attributes are already determined; her life hangs in the balance of her parents' relationship.

'Why does it mean a row? You've always had a good marriage, you two. He *would* want to know, Kate. FOC, Kate, father of the child.' Kate is irritated by the jargon. Mel blanks out the time that Rob emailed her, asked her to lunch. Wisely she had failed to take his point and bluntly told him she did not eat lunch. *He loves Kate. I am not going there.*

'Yes, he would want to know! And then he'd have an opinion and it would always coincide with the opinion of the man in the white coat. They don't talk about mothers and babies, you know, they talk about risk assessment. Anyone would think we were talking window cleaning or adventure holidays. Risk assessment! Rob doesn't want any more children, and he certainlydoesn't want a handicapped child at this stage. He's nearly fifty you know. Oh Mel! Once I have told him, I'll have to keep an open mind about whether we are having it or not until every last test has been carried out'. Mel squeezes her hand. 'And even then we wouldn't know for certain that the baby would be healthy. I can't put a baby on hold. How do people do that? I know myself. The baby and I would be growing closer every day and Rob would become the enemy. As soon as I tell him our interests will diverge. And if I don't tell him, how will I forgive him for not having known?'

'So what is your plan?' Mel's big eyes are watching her.

'Plan is rather a grand word for it. I don't really have a plan, Mel. I suppose I am just keeping quiet as long as I can and waiting to see what happens. If I am still pregnant in a month I guess we'll have to talk about it, but until then, why not keep the peace? There may be nothing to discuss.'

'Well look, do call me any time if you want to chat.' In fact, she means it.

'I will,' says Kate, meaning 'I won't'. 'Listen, thank you. We must put the phones back on now.'

'Yeah. Shame about the callers. They really muck up the morning don't they?' At that moment the doorbell rings and they go through their routine of admitting a caller to the centre. Together they leave the ops' room, both phones fortuitously off the hook already. Together they walk towards the front door and the lighted porch. Telepathically they have agreed that it is Mel who will see the caller in the interview room and Kate begins to hang back. She makes sure the visitor can see her, see that Mel is not there alone, nods to Mel as she shows the young woman into the interview room and punches the code once more into the internal set of doors. Once back in the ops' room she puts back one of the phones. There is a personal alarm in the ops' room but Kate has never seen anyone take it with them. Sams have to believe they are safe. *When the Whisperer phones at three am and says he is outside, that he knows which car is yours, that he will meet you when your shift ends, you have to believe he is lying.*

BILLY HAS HAD his supper. His food is the ever-bland, tepid fuel that nourishes the institutionally fed. Making tea is a challenge that is thought to be good for Billy. A meal presents options beyond his understanding, choices concerning combinations and times and temperatures. Too many things to hold in his head at one time. And then of course Billy is not allowed near knives. Not any more. Sheila is very strict on that one - she cannot afford any more slip-ups - and Maeve, her right-hand woman, implements Sheila's policies in her own particular way. She calls Billy 'my little lamb' which makes him laugh with fear; sometimes she hits him which makes him cry.

The institutional, politically correct, salt- and taste-free offering appears three times a day on his plate. Like an domestic animal, the times are not of his choosing. He has never known anything else except in the interlude with the Littles, with Fred and Iris. Choice and privacy are not things he remembers now. Billy eats everything he is given scrupulously. He knows that food is valuable and that the way he eats is unacceptable. Matron saw to that. Once Ray had left after that incident on the beach, Matron was vicious to Billy. She had rather fancied Ray. Billy understood that choice was for other people.

SIX

Are you the person who could care indefinitely for the disempowered? Without cruelty? Without bullying? There is nothing lovable about them. Progress, growth, change are all things that happen in other people's lives. Caring for those who will never improve is a task to test the most optimistic, the most compassionate health professional. An act of frustration committed in a dead end. Sadly Maeve was not optimistic or compassionate to begin with. Her own history left her with two choices, victim or bully and she was tired of being the victim. Outside powers have deemed it a good idea from time to time to try and normalise Billy, to rehabilitate him. The mission statement speaks of enabling and facilitating. *'What Billy needs is responsibility.'* They start with making tea. Billy mastered the tea with only third degree burns.

'Not very handy with the kettle, was yer Billy?' Maeve reports to Sheila. Sheila nods grimly. Billy, grinning stupidly with fear holds out his bandaged paw. Greater possibilities reveal only his bewilderment. Billy is not like a teenager who has never developed. Indeed he is no longer any kind of teenager. He is dangerously unaware; his past, a blank; his future, a black hole, sucking him forward. Today Billy has called the Samaritans once already. He is supposed to be in bed. He does not remember that now. He remembers Kate. He remembers his birthday. *Coming soon. Wednesday.*

Sunday evening. 2150

He dials the number. What are the odds that the single telephone in Kate's branch will ring with Billy's call? Well, it varies. Calls are transferred back to the national distribution centre if they are not answered within fifteen seconds. Billy is calling on the national number and his call will be directed according to which offices are open and which 'phones are already busy. The chances of Billy speaking to Kate again are significantly better than of an individual punter winning the lottery, but they are not good. A bookie might offer ten to one. Billy has no notion of how his call arrives at Kate's desk but he has conceived a desire to speak only to her. To go through that story again with another, perhaps less adept, listener is too frightening, too tiring. Billy could not tell you this. He just wants to speak to Kate.

'Samaritans. Can I help you?' Billy is lucky. Tonight few offices are open and the chances of his reaching Kate are high. *It's her. It is her. Kate. Don't be clumsy, Billy. Don't drop the phone. Get your tongue ready. Ready.*

'Samaritans. Can I help you?' *It's him.* 'Billy?'

'S'Billy' The voice is thick. The accent unmistakeable.

'Yes, it's Kate.' A quickening. Something is springing into independent life.

It's Billy and I am alone. 'Billy? About your birthday. Will you keep in touch with me? Until Wednesday?' *That noise means 'yes'*. She knows it means 'yes'. The hours of listening pay off now as she can interpret Billy's noises, the rise and fall of his breathing. But behind Kate the door is opening. She jumps as if she is about to be caught red-handed.

Sunday evening. 2154

Mel re-enters the ops' room, Kate freezes, then blurts into the receiver,

'So how are you feeling today?' Billy says nothing. 'A bit low, huh? ' *Don't go, Billy, for Christ's sake, don't go.* Mel extracts the card from the box file and waves it to Kate in explanation as she leaves again. Kate can bear it no longer. 'Billy? I am going to give you my number. Billy, have you got a pen?'

'Get a pen.'

Sunday evening. 2243

'Yes. You get a pen.' This is a hanging offence and Kate knows it. With excruciating slowness - Mel could return at any moment - she dictates her mobile number to her caller, thus alienating herself for ever from the Samaritan family, from all her lifelines, from all the rules. And then she does it again. And again, until she is sure that he has it and until she cannot possibly pass off what she has done as 'spur of the moment', 'confusion', 'panic' or any other self-exculpation.

'Now you call me, Billy. Call me tomorrow. OK?' She is pretty sure he has understood, has agreed.

Next Kate speaks to a man who introduces himself as the Devil, a man full of rage against his wife for leaving him, such rage, he explains that he hates all living things.

'I'm Satan, I tell you! Fallen angel! I could give you the best fuck ever. I was the best husband ever. You'd be begging me for more.'

'Is that right?' asks Kate with a certain boredom. He tries again to pick a fight. Kate is not tempted. 'You sound really unhappy. I think you're in a lot of pain.' Slowly they turn to the subject of the caller's feelings.

In the evening, if there is a bit of a lull in the telephone calls, Sams answer emails. Tonight the lull never comes and no emails are sent. At eleven she leaves Mel at the door, returning home to the absolution that only labradors can give and falling into bed unconscious. In her dreams a small child in a red coat skips to keep up.

Monday morning. 0715

WAKING IN THE Malmaison Hotel, Hull, Rob stretches his arms wide and finds empty space. How wonderful to have a whole double bed, the extravagant heat of a hotel. *And a guilt-free cooked breakfast!* No-one except himself to please for at least two hours. He loves Kate and Seb and Max. He even loves the dogs. But the small boy in him resents being an adult, resents having to consider the needs and feelings of those creatures he loves. So sometimes, he doesn't. People need a lot of comforting for their bad behaviour.

Rob drops the wet towel on the bed and wincing, slaps on cologne. He is a good-looking man of forty-seven and vain enough to care. He has a big project meeting this morning and the admin girl at the client's end has the longest legs and the shortest skirts. He wants to feel attractive today. *And powerful.* A new arts' centre in Hull has been given the green light and the finance people are pretty sure they want Rob Hurst's name on it. His small practice has suddenly become fashionable. *Some people still scratching around for a real break. The way old Chris looked at the wine label when they came to dinner. And how much time does Kate have for me? Still wrapped up in the boys, her good works, all those retreats. First thing on a Summer's morning she's out there on the lawn doing her thing, whatever that is, just when I want to feel her body next to mine. Women still look at me. Other women.* Now and again Rob has been tempted to indulge himself with someone else - the email to Mel lingers in his uneasy memory. *She was so utterly fascinating that night, so thin, so interesting. Kate in such a bad mood that I didn't feel like helping. Mel is so foreign, so single. God, the way she looked at me. It must have been months since she had sex.* What he means, of course, is that she had appeared to find him so utterly fascinating - but he is quite glad it did not happen. He blushes to remember how he led Davina on. *Poor Davina.* Rob sighs and frowns. He does not want other women, life might be simpler if he did. But he wants Kate.

Since that publicity in the weekend *FT* Rob has had a queue of clients. He will never again need to listen to people who waste his time, cramp his style, people without imagination or resources, people who do not sufficiently trust his vision. Rob is on a roll. He is thinking Beaubourg, Bilbao, Tate Modern. *I am thinking big.* The day the *FT Weekend* editor had called him to arrange a date, Rob had opened Champagne and taken Kate to bed after lunch for what she called a Big Duck Fuck. 'So now you're a big duck.' *She was not complaining*. He would rather she had said Big Dick. *Once she'd have said Big Dick.* Still, it was great in bed. *And how many men still feel that about their wives? The way she...*

The raw sexual energy that had fuelled them both at twenty-five is less plentiful now but still there. Motherhood had cleaned up her language, but fortunately her mind was as dirty as ever. As he straightens his tie in the mirror, twisting his head left and right until the collar and tie sit comfortably, Rob starts to plan a little weekend away. They have been meaning to go to Venice again for ages. Doing up his cuff-links, he moves towards the door and braces himself for life outside. *That's what she needs, a little treat.* For a moment Rob softens inside.

KATE IS AWAKE too. Stretching her arms wide she finds empty space and curls up small in disappointment. She hugs Rob's pillow to her and remembers what it feels like to have a pregnant belly as big as the pillow. She remembers her dream and turns her thoughts away. *Much too early. Go back to sleep.*

Monday morning 0805

MEL IS IN her bathroom listening to *Today* as she does her make-up and going over what Kate said in her head. *How would I feel? Pregnant at forty-five.* Briefly she mourns her ex-husband, Frank. *The call from Billy? What would I do? I made it sound easy when I was talking to Kate.* Mel has always toed the policy line but then she has never been pushed that far.

BARKING.THAT MUST be the postman. Every dog's friend. I must have a pee. Nothing on my phone. No missed calls.

Thank God. Rob. I wish you were here. Sometimes it seemed she had been saying that for twenty years.

BILLY IS AWAKE too. *Got her number now. After breakfast. 'You call me'. They don't usually say that. They say 'Call again if you need to. There is always somebody here'. 'You call me'. She said that. Kate. Kate said that. She calls me Billy. Like Dorothy.* The names make his head swim and the bad feeling begins.

Monday morning. 0915

KATE IS RUSHING to get to her weekly therapist appointment with Sue. Billy has not called. She had her 'phone next to her as she cleaned her teeth this morning. *Am I hoping he will ring or hoping he won't? What if he calls while I'm with Sue?*
She notices how this anxiety loops around in her head so that the guilt and fear she feels about having given him her number - *what was I thinking?* - are all contained now in this worry that he will call and she will not be able to answer. For years she felt that therapy was just self-indulgence. Six months in, she knows it is hard work.

Sue lives in a large cottage in a village about twenty minutes away. A friend had recommended her and Kate began seeing her in a crisis as people often do. T he feelings that arose as her children became adults were dominating her life. They were feelings of apprehension, panic, really, and a question mark as to who she herself was to become. This was a question Kate had delayed answering twenty years ago by having children. Now it was back to haunt her. As she prepares for this meeting she has small twinges of guilt and delight - a new baby will put off examining those feelings for still more years. She feels as though she has had a sentence commuted, as though by lucky fluke she has escaped some punishment that had been hanging over her. At the same time she realizes that the rite of passage has simply receded into the future. *I wonder what Sue will think of me. In another life I would like Sue as a friend.*

'What *I* will think of you?' repeats Sue. She sits, small and brown in her kelim armchair reminding Kate of a nutmeg. The room has a spicy smell. Kate laughs, embarrassed,

'Yes. You know, I felt guilty about being pregnant...as though I don't deserve it.'

'So what is that about? What is it about deserving things?' *Being honest is such hard work!*

Sue does not engage her about Billy or the baby. She is rarely interested in what she calls 'the story' and this can be frustrating. Rather, Sue asks Kate to talk about her own feelings and thoughts about these new aspects of her life.

'What is the feeling, Kate? What is it about a new baby that is so attractive?'

She especially asks her whether these feelings remind her of any previous situations. And of course they do. To Kate's horror, they do. She knows the apprehension with which she awaits Rob's reaction to the baby. *I know that feeling I get when he disagrees with me - that the thing I want must be wrong.*

'I feel I am a bad person to want what I want. I cannot enjoy having what I want unless the other person approves.' *If it was the right thing to want, the other person would want the same wouldn't they?* Even Kate can spot Marilyn's work here as she describes how she feels. Compassion arises in her for the bitter efforts of her younger self to move her mother to affection, and for the disappointment. She is in tears now and she wipes them away with the back of her hand, casting her eyes to the ceiling and struggling to control her voice. Within her a cluster of cells is dividing as fast as it can. Arm buds are twice the size they were a few days ago. The baby will have blond hair, like the boys, like her brothers.

'Kate... That desire is not right or wrong; it just is.' *The desire is not right or wrong; it just is.* 'Can you allow that?' Sue's eyes are warm and Kate feels her heart open.

IT WAS A couple of weeks ago that Kate got into the car to drive to town for her a Samaritan duty and a small death awaited her on the road. She is naturally sanguine about road conditions and is therefore disconcerted to drive straight into a traffic jam on the dual carriage-way which usually speeds her into the nearby town. *Not more roadworks!* She has left no extra time for emergencies like this and hears immediately the accusing voice within. *Just typical of you, Kate Walker! No consideration! Someone else can pick up the pieces, I suppose!* Gently squeezing the brake and drawing up behind a lorry proclaiming itself a *Big Green Parcel Machine*, Guiltily glancing around for police cars, she picks up her mobile from the tray beneath the dash and dials the Samaritan office to leave a message on the office phone - *'on my way, but delayed'*. She checks the time. *Nine o'clock.* Whoever is coming on duty with her should pick up that message about twenty-past when they sign in.

The traffic eases itself off the slip road and into the congestion of the dual carriageway. Kate's mind is passing the time without her by silently pronouncing the names on the foreign container lorries when suddenly the cars in front of her pick up speed. But this is a temporary relief because just ahead there is another disruption; something is in the road. Kate's heart races but even so her mind is faster, recklessly interpreting what it sees in the light of what she fears..*Not roadworks.* No reassuring yellow lights broadcasting an innocuous explanation. This is not the everyday irritation of lane closure, white line painting, resurfacing. This something is taking drivers by surprise. Cars are swerving past something, some lumpy thing lying, clothes flapping, in the road; they chicane in and out of their lanes to avoid it, whatever it is; whoever it is. No more doubt now; blood on the clothes; someone in the road; a body in the road, maybe more than one. Kate feels faint.

No-one can stop as the flow of traffic is too thick, moving, though agonisingly slowly for someone in a hurry, with too much momentum. It can only be a matter of moments before someone fails to react in time, before someone's dexterity is overstretched and the traffic charges directly onward, over rather than around the fragile thing that lies there. Suddenly driving seems the most dangerous thing in the world and, one hand on her baby, Kate pulls onto the hard shoulder and turns the air conditioning on full, closing her eyes. Her body remembers another occasion years ago, frosty bodies propped against a wall, and is inexplicably overwhelmed by nausea, fear, resentment and guilt. *Why didn't she love me?*

Kate opens her eyes and permits present reality to enter. She watches the cars dancing in and out of the inside lane fifty yards away. She holds her breath as the bloodied clothes, *no, not clothes,* pieces of fabric, red, white and floral, flap around the inert, person-sized bundle just inches away from juggernaut wheels. As her panic abates her eyes can see what is there : a lorry has earlier shed its load of fabrics and careered on its way unknowing. *That is all it is - rags, bundles of rags!*There is no body, no creature being tortured to a slow death by the casual touch of giant wheels. Her mind bursts with a shout of triumph back into the twenty-first century, back into the present. Her body abandons its unwanted, patterned response. *Everything's OK!* For now. Under the warmth of her hand, deep within her womb, a tiny presence relaxes.

The cars, bikes, vans and lorries which make up this morning's commuters are co-operatively and cheerfully negotiating their path, at minimum speed, she now sees, around the stumbling block. She rejoins the fray and within minutes her breathing has returned to normal and she is back on schedule. The traffic lights are forgiving and a parking space materialises outside the Samaritans' front door. As she checks her watch and types in the door code to enter, she sees it is nine twenty-five.

Kate enters the ops' room at nine thirty-five, picks up her mail from the pigeon hole and smiles at Bryony who looks up from the rota and smiles back.

'Sorry, Bad traffic.'

'Don't worry. You're fine,' says Bryony magnanimously.

'Coffee?' *A peace offering.*

'Tea, please. Milk, no sugar.' *Resistance*. Bryony voice becomes a voice off as Kate goes out to the kettle, but years of school-teaching and amateur dramatics have honed Bryony's diction and Kate does not miss a word. 'I'm just trying to find someone to cover next Thursday for me. I've made a bit of a bish.'

'Aha?'

Bryony is a smart woman of sixty-eight or so. She dresses neatly but always with a flash of colour that Kate enjoys. Today the neat cream top and navy trousers are touched here and there with emerald green - a silk scarf, shoes and rather good enamel earrings. Her still dark hair and pleasing face are well looked-after and she is easy to like. When she is not taking care of her beloved Ian, whose every want is her priority, she martials the rest of her considerable energy into wresting from the local dramatic society first class productions of the less demanding classics. Often the proceeds enrich the Samaritans - each branch must raise its own funds and is self-supporting.

Standing in the passage making the tea a memory takes Kate back to 1988.

Edward and Davina in London. The year the twins started school. An Inspector Calls - all proceeds to the Samaritans.

Kate's friend Anna was a Samaritan back then. Kate had not started. Rob was not keen.

'Can't we just buy the tickets? Do we actually have to go? Just give Anna the money. Make a donation.'

'It might be fun. I sort of promised.'

'Oh no. Amateur dramatics. Not my idea of a night out, darling. Poor old Anna may have nothing else to do - *he means she is single* - but honestly Kate, can't you get involved with something a bit more...'

'A bit more what?' Kate's voice grew thin. Silence. 'Please, Rob. Just this once?' And they do go.

MEANWHILE IN LIVERPOOL Billy is having his tea and watching *Coronation Street*. Fred and Iris are having a walk in the pleasant warmth of the July evening. The blossom trees are out in their road and the doctor has said Fred must walk more.

ROB CAME WITH her to the play.

'You're a sweet little thing. Very earnest, aren't you, about Things That Matter?' Kate wondered why she wanted to bite him when he was being so nice. The play was being given in a Kensington garden. A pergola did duty as the bar. The house was smart and the garden was packed. Rob cheered up. Kate is having a good time. The play is really entertaining.

'Hi Anna, there you are.' Anna, plain and earnest, has made her way to Kate's side. 'Rob, here's Anna.' She turned to speak to him but he was smiling and waving at her from the makeshift bar across the lawn. He stood with a man in his late fifties, handsome, wealthy. It was a look that Rob aspired to. Edward, it turned out, was on the board of The Colosseum. His path had crossed Rob's at some long-ago function but Rob was not one to forget a face - *just the sort of contact Selwyn Hurst & Co. needs.*

'Look who's here, Kate!' He was beaming at her proudly in a way that, she knew, had nothing to do with her. It turned out that Edward and Mrs Edward were lending what the programme called their 'lovely home' for the production. 'Brilliant effort, Davina', he said addressing Mrs Edward. *As if the woman had put on the production single-handed rather than paid the gardners to put out a few chairs.* Kate hated it when Rob was his public self. She could hear his laugh pursue her through the small crowd as she went to find the loo. When Rob was like this Kate shrank into herself and did not know him. Well, at least that is what it felt like.

Mrs Edward had the grey blond hair and race-horse legs of her class. Her size eight rib-cage was perfect for the tiny cashmere cardigan and the price of her discreet diamond studs would have kept the Samaritans going for years. Hers was a look Kate envied and had no chance of emulating. *Not without surgery, anyhow.* Mrs Edward's understanding smile was the kind Kate had learned not to trust, the kind that did not find Kate and her strange, spiritual ways 'quite the thing, Edward'. Kate hated her on sight. She made her feel like a cart-horse and a slightly below average cart-horse at that. *When will I lose the weight from carrying the twins?* 'Poor Rob', she could see Davina thinking. She was wearing her prettiest Summer dress and a dove grey pashmina but as Davina and Rob looked her up and down, Kate began to feel sorry for her husband too. Davina was the kind of wife Rob should have had; she positively glowed in the public eye.

Rob and Davina hit it off in a big way. They were thirsty for more drink and Kate could see that the admiration they showered on each other was something they missed in their own partners. Kate and Rob did not get away without a luncheon invitation to their place in Berkshire and Kate's heart sank as she saw another Sunday going in the service of Rob's career. Well, she presumed it was his career. *I mean, Davina must be fifty....*

'What about the children?' she had hissed desperately at Rob and to her embarrassment, Rob had not heard her but Edward had. Taking her gently by the arm, he turned her away from their respective partners and moved her purposefully towards the rose garden. She noticed Edward was drinking water.

'Bring them. No really,' - he saw Kate's horrified expression - 'Davina would love you to come down to *Badgers.' It would be Badgers!* 'Between you and me, I think she's quite smitten with your husband - and I would love to meet your children. Twins, yes? Boys. Rob was saying. They'd love it.' Kate blushed an even deeper shade. *Was my instant dislike of this charming man's wife very obvious? Imagine Seb and Max here in this immaculate garden running riot through the roses.* She only had time to mumble an answer before Davina and Rob were upon them and the second half began. Under cover of darkness Kate began to imagine her sons climbing on the antique stonework and dripping ice-cream on the white calico that *Badgers* was certain to provide.

'Now there's someone you could make a real friend of,' said Rob, at the wheel as ever, on the way home. 'What a woman! Do you know she ran her own business as well as keeping two houses going?' Kate blushed again, with anger this time. *I can just imagine the kind of business the fragile Davina runs and how much housework she does. With those nails! Per..lease!*

'Perhaps she has help.' But Rob was enchanted and she is wasting her breath. Actually, thought Kate maliciously as she lay awake listening to her husband's alcoholic snores, it was not even Davina, it was the money that fascinated him. *Who was it that was seduced by a shower of gold coins?*

THE WRETCHED DAY has arrived for Kate and she dresses the boys in their best French outfits and alternately threatens and bribes them in the car.

'Just this once, boys. Please, be good. For Mummy.' There was still a pre-school wildness, a terrible freedom about them which struck terror into Kate's heart as she thought of the ordeal ahead. Marilyn had from time to time made plain her opinion of her unbiddable grandsons. They needed a firm male hand, preferably on the bottom, and of course, she added, Rob was never there and Kate was far too weak. So that was that. It was on Sundays like this that Kate in her heart thought her mother was right.

Edward and Davina are in the kitchen, preparing.

'Are you OK, darling?' Davina is frenetically busy putting out meringues and party poppers.

'Absolutely! '

'Was it wise to ask them?'

'Oh Edward, don't be ridiculous. Why on earth not? It's six years ago. I can't hide indefinitely.' He went to put his arms round her but she kept moving on her busy path from fridge to table, to larder and back.

'Where's Mrs Williams?'

'She'll be here about one.'

'Take it easy, darling.' He can sense her hysteria building and he does not know how to help her.

IN THE CAR on the way to Berkshire the twins are intrigued and unsettled by the atmosphere. Their parents are tense. The day ahead already contained a frisson of danger and they were curious to see what would transpire. They were always at their very worst when someone put on a show for them. They knew when to say 'thank you' well enough but they were still wise enough to see when there was nothing to be grateful for - just adults trying to impress each other.

Davina had made a 'special effort' and the twins spotted straight off that Mummy and Davina were not on the same side. They sat on a green velvet lawn as Edward brought out the Champagne into the garden, Davina offered mini cans of Coke glistening with condensation in their own ice bucket. Mummy smiled through gritted teeth. Coke did not feature in the boys' daily diet.

'Just one, Max, there's a good boy. Ummm, actually Davina...' But she had lost them. Max's eyes lit up and he took two and refused to say thank you. Davina smiled at the little boy and then, pityingly, at Kate.

'Oh dear, Max. Don't you know how to say thank you? Let's see what a meringue can do?' Max, catching his twin's eye, knew they were on a roll. 'I bet you'd like a meringue,' wheedled Davina, her eyes still on Kate's mortified face. *Poor red-faced creature. Rob could have done a lot better than that.* Kate's horrified protestations - *It's nearly lunch-time! He hasn't said thank you for the Coke yet!* - were drowned in the twins' roar of approval. And so the day proceeded with every new outrage on the children's part rewarded by Davina. Kate had to keep thanking Davina for undermining all her attempts to control her own children. Rob was busy talking.

'Ice cream! Oh you are lucky, aren't you, boys? You are kind, Davina.'

You cow! 'Say 'thank you', boys.' But they were off. When Seb spat his out, Davina offered him another flavour and gave the offending ice to the dog. When the children could consume no more, Davina flopped into an antique garden chair next to Rob as if to say she had done her duty with his sons and their dull mother and now he could spoil her. Rob was thrilled. He turned from his conversation with Edward and gave her his full attention. Kate remembered how attractive he was when he did that. Ten years later Davina was dead but right then Kate hated her.

'Well, you certainly have a way with children, Davina,' said Rob as he passed her a glass. Edward was looking hard at his wife but she was making eyes at their guest. Kate thought she might explode. Rob appeared not to notice the boys' dreadful progress; he looked the other way and smiled a lot at Davina, tousling the children's hair as they passed his chair. Kate felt ridiculous and mean.

DADDY'S ON DAVINA'S side, then. The twins were getting the hang of this. They avoided their mother's eye. Edward, having welcomed his guests and dealt with the drinks, had disappeared, with many apologies, to take a phone call. Rob, Davina and Kate sat on white calico under a parasol chatting and sipping Champagne. They talked about Hong Kong where Kate had never been.

KATE HAD WORN the wrong thing. The smart thing but the wrong thing. She knew that as soon as they got out of the car and saw Davina in her faded denim shirt and white capri pants, comfortable old tennis shoes on her beautiful brown feet.

'Sorry, darling, I've been gardening,' she said, indicating her clothes and kissing Rob first. Kate was too smart and too hot. 'I love the sun,' purred Davina undoing another button of the faded denim. She wore an old straw hat that made her look thirty.

'Me too,' agreed Rob. His eyes never left her. 'I'm afraid I don't get outside enough. Look at your lovely tan.'

'But you obviously keep yourself in shape.' Davina ran an appreciative hand over his upper arm.

'The odd game of squash...' The twins were hypnotised. They had never seen Daddy like this before. They set off to trample the flowerbeds. Rob was still being lionised by Davina and Kate had to run after them. She felt ridiculous. Her face was an unflattering beetroot and the smile on her face was painfully tight, worse each time she sat down after a run-in with a child. Rob seemed not to notice Kate getting up every three minutes and Davina smiled at her each time she sat down again.

'You are a busy mum, aren't you?' Kate's smile waned. Seb tried to torture the Jack Russell which threatened to bite him.

'What a shame!' exclaimed Davina, 'A little boy who does not like dogs! Her glance made it plain which parent she blamed for this moral failing.' Max threw his Coke can in the pond 'for the fishes' . Rob and Davina raised their eyebrows at each other and Kate rushed to pick the can out. Now her best jumper (dry clean only) had pond water on it. *Why the fuck did I wear this?* Max hung onto her leg as she marched back to the table and Seb ran round them both making farting noises. Kate smiled harder.

'...not at home as much as I should be, I'm afraid,' Rob was saying as she came back red in the face, having fought Max off her. Her best shoes were hurting and Max had laddered her tights. Her smile was frozen. The boys were mutinous.

Now Seb wanted to go to the loo. "For a poo" he added seriously and then both boys fell on the lawn with hysterics. Kate stood up and took his hand in a terrifying grip. He knew that grip. When she bent down and spoke gently to him, the grip on his wrist spoke louder. *Mum's getting stressy.*

'Do you really need the loo, Seb?'

'Into the hall, turn left,' sang Davina without looking. *Oh do take those wretched children away!* As Kate crossed the lawn with a recalcitrant Seb in her grasp she heard, 'A spot more, Rob? We seem to have lost our spouses.'

'Let me look after you, Davina.' Over her shoulder Kate saw her hold out her glass for him to fill. As she leaned forward a fine tanned cleavage revealed itself. *Gardening clothes, my arse,* thought Kate with unwonted rudeness. The ankles were on show too as Davina took off her shoes and now sat with arms hugging her knees, feet up on her chair. *The way only thin people do.* Meanwhile Max was following Mummy with a view to rescuing Seb from that grip he recognised. Kate was close to tears. Anger and humiliation rose in her and for a moment she thought of throwing her wretched children into the car and driving back to London. *Bloody well leave them to it.* She hoped only Max could hear as Seb protested 'Mummy, you're hurting my hand!' and Kate more or less dragged him up the steps onto the terrace and through the French windows into the hall. It was a beautiful room with a baby grand and a parquet floor. Family photos covered the piano lid and flowered armchairs nestled in a corner. A couple of Regency dining chairs with striped silk seats stood against the wall.

Now Seb was chanting to himself 'Poo, Poo, Poo, Poo!' under his breath; Max took up the cry. They were full to the eyebrows with refined sugar and caffeine and not about to call a halt now.

'Seb! What is going on? Max?' pleaded Kate in a hoarse voice, squatting down beside them. The chanting got louder and they danced away from her. 'Why are you being so naughty? ' Now they were shouting, 'Poo! You're a poo! You're a poo! Poo! Poo!' A terrible crash sent a bowl of roses to the floor. Broken glass, water and flowers surrounded them and Kate collapsed on a chair, finally crying. Her face was in her hands, mascara on her hectic cheeks, her painful shoes kicked aside and that was when Edward came out of his study and Kate thought she might die.

'NOW BOYS!' EDWARD'S voice was calm, affectionate and commanding, 'I think you have had enough excitement.' Magically the housekeeper had appeared at his elbow and somehow the broken glass was already safely in a bag, the roses in her other hand.

'The water will soon dry.'

'Say you are sorry to your mother and go with Mrs Williams to the kitchen. You need some water and I think we have some puzzles in there to keep you busy.'

Max and Seb knew immediately that the game was up. They looked at their shoes and murmured 'Sorry, Mummy'.

'Good,' said Mrs Williams and they disappeared after her, quite grateful that the spoiling had stopped, anxious to feel good again and to please someone.

'Now then,' said Edward, 'what do *you* need? I am so sorry, I've been on the telephone. Unforgivable. ' Kate had scrambled to her feet and put on her shoes as fast as the twins had gone quiet. *How can this lovely man be married to the hideous Davina?*

'Erm, I think I could do with some water too, actually.' She sat in a flowered armchair with a cool breeze on her hot cheeks whilst Edward fetched water for them both. Something about the way he carried the jug in one hand and their two glasses in the other made Kate feel very close to him, special.

'I am so sorry,' she started.

'Yes, of course,' said Edward, 'and I am sorry too.'

'You! It's my children that are behaving hideously.'

'Yes, me. I should have headed Davina off before you came. I could see what was going to happen. Children are a problem for her, you see. She's got them into this state, hasn't she?' He looked down sadly and considered how much more to say. 'Rob tells me you are interested in the Samaritans. You'd make a good one, I'll bet.'

'Um, when the boys are a bit bigger,' said Kate apologetically and waited.

Perhaps they could not have children. Decisively Edward got up and went to the piano. He returned with two photographs, each in a beautiful frame. 'This was our son,' he said holding out a picture of an angelic boy of five or six with Davina's green eyes and Edward's chin. 'He died.'

'What was his name,' asked Kate, for want of anything else to say.

'Jamie.'

'What a beautiful boy.'

'Yes, he was a beautiful boy, our only child, until he was about sixteen; funny, clever, sporty. I just about managed to stop Davina spoiling him to death.' A terrible pause as they both heard what he had said. Edward grimaced, raised his eyebrows at his own indelicacy and with a sigh, passed his right palm in a circle across his forehead and gazed into the distance.

'But he died anyway, I'm afraid.' Edward is massaging the back of his neck with his hand, pacing slowly, gazing at the patterned rug. 'He got very depressed in his last two years at school but we did not notice.' Edward exhales in such a way that Kate feels the sharp freshness of the self-recrimination. He holds out the other photo. 'Here he is just after his GCSEs. I've always thought you can already see a shadow across his face. ' Kate is looking into the guarded, green eyes of a good-looking young man in a polo shirt. He is sitting in a chair that Kate's husband now occupies under the parasol. Davina, then as now, gazes across in adoration.

'We did not know how to distinguish depression from normal teenage behaviour. Apparently that's very common. By the time he was at university he tried to kill himself. One night he locked himself in his room in hall with paracetamol and a bottle of whisky. But he failed. Friends got him out, called an ambulance, got his stomach pumped, the works, you know.'

Kate nodded and let him continue.

'He needed treatment when he came out of hospital; he started his first year again. The university were very good but the psychiatrist wasn't. One drug after another did not suit him and he began to choose his own drugs - to 'self-medicate', isn't that what they call it? I suppose he'd already tried stuff at school but Davina won't hear of it. She maintains a fiction that he was led astray. Ecstasy, cocaine and eventually heroin. Jamie was not the kind of boy to be led astray. My son killed himself as surely as if he had put a bullet through his head. And he made us watch. That was the new part. Where before he was discreet, secretive if you like, suddenly he wanted us to know how much he was suffering. He wanted to see us suffer too. At first the drugs made him more outgoing, we thought he was getting better, but slowly the truth dawned. He was committed to dying and eventually, when he was twenty, he managed it. We don't know why and I cannot forgive him for making his mother watch. I live with my anger, my bewilderment and of course, my grief. I loved him very much.'

Edward sat down abruptly. Kate nodded again but did not speak. Briefly she put her hand on his and lowered her eyes to the rug where his eyes were fixed once more. They sat in silence until he spoke again. 'So Davina finds visiting children very painful.' He looks into Kate's eyes. 'She is crucified with guilt, as all parents of suicides are, I'm told. She still feels we could have given more.' Edward turned to stare into the garden. His frustration is tangible; his voice falls. 'I know we should have given less.' Now he is smiling at Kate, who feels his pain in her own heart and sees it around his eyes.

'How long ago?'

'Jamie would have been twenty-six a few weeks ago.'

'Oh, I'm so sorry. I can't think of anything more terrible.'

'No.' At length he spoke again; a lighter tone. 'One more thing, Kate. You have been kind enough to let me open my heart to you.'

'Yes?'

'Let me tell you something, Kate. He's behaving like an idiot today, Davina has that effect on people, but Rob loves you very much, you know.' Kate felt her face prick again as she glanced up at him from beneath her eyebrows.

'I...'

'Young men are often not great husbands - I know I wasn't - but he talks about you such a lot and the way he looks at you speaks for itself. Perhaps you don't notice?' Kate is surprised to hear herself admit,

'Since the twins were born, I have not been a great wife. I just fell head over heels in love with them, I'm afraid and Rob must have felt pushed out.'

'Don't worry, that will change, said Edward, putting the photos back on the piano. Shall we go and brave lunch?' Kate smiled and got up. Sensing a question in her minute hesitation, he added, 'Don't worry about the boys. Mrs Williams will have them eating out of her hand by now. Oh, just a tick.' He darted out into the hall and returned in two steps with a large sunhat. 'There you are, try this. See? Even more delicious than before.' Edward had a very flirtatious smile from twenty years ago.

After that the day had gone extraordinarily well. She now saw Davina with Edward's eyes and she looked quite different to Kate. Who could envy her thinness now? *Or her money*? When her own dear boys rushed back into the garden later quite returned to their generous, loving selves, Kate felt a surge of compassion for Davina even as she saw her make eyes at Rob. From time to time she made eye contact herself with her husband and, it was true, he did look at her with pride and with love. As they went in to lunch he came up behind her, kissed her neck and whispered,

I can't wait to get home. Your breasts are irresistible in that top.'

SEVEN

'BUT THEY'RE not English, are they?' Bryony is persisting. She has read in this morning's *Telegraph* about the radical teaching in some of Britain's mosques. Poor Ian's operation had been delayed by queue-jumping asylum seekers, according to his wife.

'Of course they're English, Bryony,' begins Kate, but fortunately the phone rings.

Soon Bryony is on a call and Kate is alone at the computer. Once upon a time she used to sign off emails 'with love' but someone had complained. They thought it unsuitable and Kate was told to stop. Yet what else was it, she mused, that brought her and the other volunteers into this office once a week to listen to the afflicted and the despairing? What else could it be, but love? Signing off was the most difficult part in many ways. Kate refused to adopt the meaningless 'Take care', the saccherine 'We are here for you'. Policy was against 'Keep in touch' (encourages dependence). Sometimes, in silent protest, she simply put 'Jo'.

Monday afternoon 1500

THAT AFTERNOON KATE sees Sue. Billy still has not called.

'Well maybe you will hear no more,' she says, when Kate has told her the whole story, her mixed feelings over what she has done. 'It sounds as though your own fears have been triggered by his story. What are you afraid of?' *What am I afraid of? Good question.* They talk a lot then about the child she lost, her fury at Marilyn who had engineered the secret birth, the adoption.

'Interesting that Billy's call has brought up all these feelings about children, isn't it? What's happening now?'

Monday evening 2130

IT IS THE fifteenth of December and the Christmas decorations in town have been up since Remembrance Day. Nigel, the gardner, is bringing the tree tomorrow and Kate anticipated decorating her beautiful house. The box of decorations stands ready in the hall. It is a long time since the twins wanted to do this. *All those home-made crackers. Pasta shapes with glitter. Dodgy angels.* Kate loved that time of her life but it is quite nice to be able to do it herself without humouring the under sixes. Standing in the hall, she thinks of another little soul who might want to help in a few years' time. She feels apprehensive - *am I too old, too selfish?* - but also ecstatically happy.

And there is another thing. This time she is sure it will be a girl. *Leila.* A few weeks ago when she had done the test twice because she could not believe the result, Kate had seen Leila playing out there on the lawn. The sun is very bright and low; this December morning looks like a Summer afternoon, long shadows stretching down to the river. *She is only just visible in the brilliance, but, yes, there she is playing with her tea-set under the horse chestnut tree, the daughter I never had. I was scared to have daughters. Scared of failing to love them. When my sons came I was over the moon. Each of them was a gift that I could hold in my arms, someone, at last, who could bear all the love I had to give.*

Kate is planning an early night when Billy calls. Her phone is ringing as she steps out of the shower and thinking 'Rob' she lunges to take the call.

'Rob?' Silence. 'Hello? ' Kate clutches her towel around her, trying to dry herself and hold the mobile at the same time. Silence. Her movements slow down and stop as she listens to the empty line. *Oh God, what have I done?* 'Hello?' At the other end her name is pronounced by someone whose tongue was not ready. *There were not the three rings, you see. No-one said 'Samaritans. Can I help you?' How can you begin if no-one says 'Samaritans. Can I help you?' How do you know what to say?*

Billy has never made a telephone call to a private number. Kate's number is folded so small that the paper is soft, the number nearly illegible. Someone had to show him how to use the mobile. 'Gorra girlfriend, Billy?' Now his large form is scrunched up against the coffee machine; he wishes he knew how to speak quietly.

'Billy?' *My heart is like lead. What have I done? There is no-one I can tell.*

'Billy. It's Kate. Billy? Can I help you?' Billy relaxes. *'Samaritans. Can I help you?'* It is nearly the same. It will do.

'My birthday.'

'I know.'

'Go to the park.'

'I know. Sefton Park.'

'Park.'

'Billy? I am worried that you will get into trouble.'

'Trouble.'

'Yes, with Dorothy.'

'Met Dorothy in the park.'

'I know.'

'Bin naughty with the little girl.' All at once, Kate sees again the police cordon, the grieving parents. Fear grips her. She can no longer hover near the abyss but must plunge over. Anything but this disabling vertigo. Along an internal path, a large figure is approaching, bundled up against the wind.

'You said. ' She jumps. 'Billy? Can I come? To the park? ' She is falling. They have left the script. The uncharted seas of Billy's life have just grown wilder and less manageable. The make-shift coracle of his daily 'phone call has hit an iceberg. Fear makes him laugh. Kate thinks herself encouraged. She speaks quickly now, desperate to feel her feet hit the ground. 'Where shall I meet you, Billy? Near the glass-house? Is that where you go? Meet the girls on their way to school and take them to the glass-house? Do you know the glass-house, Billy?'

'Glass-house. Dorothy.' Billy's tongue is in such confusion, he can manage no more. Kate's decision is made.

'Look for me there, Billy. I'll be at the glass-house about a quarter to nine.'

Billy hangs up. They are both in shock. Kate saves the number from which he called. Billy exists on her 'phone now. *A mobile number. Untraceable.*

Tuesday morning 1012

Kate's house does not have near neighbours but, over the bridge and across the lane is Mrs Morris's cottage. Christine or Mrs-If-I-Were-You as the boys used to call her. Christine is not much older than Kate, small, endlessly cheerful. She comes to clean for Kate and steps in whenever she can, to help with the dogs or, earlier, with the children. Now their conversation always includes an update on Sebastian and Max's progress. To Christine their lives and Kate's are as exotic as the pineapple which, in her family, used to signal the beginning of Advent. It arrived each Christmas from South Africa in blue tissue paper, the annual reminder of Uncle Richard who had emigrated with his family. Christine has views on pineapple as on most things. 'They can put it in supermarkets all they like, but what I say is, once a year was enough with pineapple'. Kate agrees out of habit. On the whole, it is easier to agree. She is, as Seb cruelly remarked, always on 'transmit' rather than 'receive'. There is no point in discussing things for long.

Christine is very fond of the dogs and has Views which she shares about how often they should be wormed, their claws clipped, and how far and how often they should be walked. 'You'll be needing the vet to that one.' Kate often feels very inadequate listening to Christine but it does not take long for her to recover. Christine is in no way malicious and seems to regard Kate as a bit slapdash - one of her favourite words - but none the worse for that. In short, Kate is the kind of laid-back, middle-class person with a life only just this side of chaotic who furnishes Christine's life with its twin pillars of work and gossip. She loves them equally.

It must take an extraordinary effort, but she makes no comment when Kate rolls up this Monday morning and explains she has to go away for twenty-four hours and can Christine look after the dogs? Christine pulls the strings of her blue apron into a sharper bow behind her and agrees.

'That'll be fine. I'm popping over to see my Mum this afternoon but they'll be alright for an hour or so, won't they?

'Of course. Put them back in the garden after lunch tomorrow, would you Christine, when you feed them?' Kate contemplates a world where popping over to see your Mum is part of daily life. *It must be nice.*

When John Morris comes home that evening and finds Keeper and Bracken in residence, he agrees with his wife that it is 'par for the course' and there is no disapproval in this expression. He merely acknowledges that their own orderly and modest existence, holidays booked well in advance for the regulation two weeks in July at the B & B in Paignton, is not shared by the rest of the world. He cannot understand these modern lives without plan or pattern. *And not for want of money, either*. Christine and John's year is reminiscent of a royal progress and each year is a carbon copy of the previous one. Spontaneity is a dubious pleasure in their book. Kate thinks they may be right.

Kate returns to the Mill House and is about to book a taxi to the station when she changes her mind. Something about driving the substantial four-wheel drive gives her a spurious sense of security. On foot she feels vulnerable and whatever happens in Liverpool, she would rather have her own car there. *A place to watch from. A place to retreat to. A get-away vehicle. If I leave now, I can spend the night in Liverpool and be in Sefton Park at eight thirty tomorrow. Billy's birthday. Shall I call Rob? Andy? My mother? I should tell someone where I'm going. Oh, Edward, where are you?* For many years Edward and Davina had been close friends but when Davina died Edward had gone to live with his brother in Spain. Kate really misses him. *What about the tree? I'll call Nigel and ask him to leave it outside.* But that seems to bring up complications. Billy is a danger to himself but not to Kate surely? Her risks are all within planted long ago by her family and nurtured over the years by Kate herself; they are the very taste of herself, the landscape she lives with. She imagines that there is no-one she can tell where she is going without facing a barrage of criticism and questions. So she just goes.

TUESDAY MIDDAY PROVES a good time to travel. Kate plugs her iPod into the stereo and listens to Bill Bryson all the way to Birmingham. On the M6 a torrential rain begins which blinds her and slows her down. Breathing deliberately into the mounting panic inside, she pulls over into the slow lane, relaxes her stomach, her shoulders, thinks about the baby. *Nearly two o'clock. If I stop here and buy something to eat in the car I can listen to The Archers.* Getting back into the car with an M & S sandwich, she hears her mobile ring. But she is fighting with a small umbrella with water soaking into her boots and dripping inevitably down the inside of her coat collar. By the time she has secured her coffee and located her phone, she sees a missed call from Rob. She does not know what she is going to say but rings back anyway. *Too late. He was between meetings. I've missed him.* His phone goes straight to voicemail. She leaves a message as light in tone as she can manage.

'I'm out and about today, sweetie.' *Well, that's true anyway.* 'See you at home tomorrow.' Then she hears the message he has left her. It is just a 'hello' but his voice makes her happy. She realises she is much more tired than she thought. The combination of the night duty and the baby are catching up with her. She eats her lunch and tilts her seat back to sleep before continuing the drive. The afternoon play provides a background to her dozing and it is nearly four by the time she starts the engine again. The sky has cleared and the road shines after its thorough wash by the rain.

Tuesday evening 1805

It has been dark for more than an hour as she leaves the motorway. She drives past her old University hall of residence, and feels a surge of adrenalin. North Mossley Hill Road - a place where good things happened to her.*And when they didn't, I did not automatically blame myself. How has this happened?* She drives around the park road but it is too dark to get her bearings. Then she sees the glass-house looking more like Crystal Palace than the broken-down greenhouse she remembers. It is lit up and clearly some festivity is taking place there. Cars and the people getting out of them indicate a party.

BILLY IS EATING another institutional meal. Iris used to cook him sausages, fried bread, baked beans, stew and dumplings. Love on a plate. There is no pleasure in food now and no love either. He is confused about tomorrow. He liked the idea of speaking to Kate but it was more difficult than he had thought. *Ring one, ring two, ring three and 'Samaritans. Can I help you?'* That's what was meant to happen. It was different standing by the coffee machine and trying to make his mouth work. *She did not say the right things.* Billy likes to talk about the park and Maeve won't let him. *Why does she ask me about it? Why does Kate want to hear about Dorothy?* Sheila says 'that's why you're fuckin' here Billy, under my feet. You're not safe to be let out. You an' yer precious Iris, precious Dorothy'. Maeve says 'we don't need to talk about that now, Billy'. He does not like things to be different and what Kate said was too different. It was not what he meant at all. It started being different when she asked him to call her. *They never do that, Samaritans, otherwise you don't get the ring one, ring two, ring three. You don't get the 'Samaritans. Can I help you?'*

KATE PARKS HER car and wanders along the path to the glass-house. She is surprised how much colder it is here and wraps her coat around her more securely. *The North.* Women with very little on clutch men in hired evening dress as they make their way to the entrance. *They never did stint on the glamour.* Potato-faced security guards lounge in the freezing wind and smile indulgently at these sirens and their escorts. They have seen it all. The historic Palm House has become a sought-after venue and tonight guests at Lorraine and Mark's engagement party are enjoying the scene. There are tealights in profusion inside mirroring the stars above. Lorraine's father made a mint in plant hire and he is delighted to provide lavishly for his daughter. Mark has a lot to live up to.

The smell of scent, smoke and alcohol escape whenever the doors swing open. Fathers and sons in unaccustomed formal dress are coming outside to smoke; here and there beneath the penguin suits a tattoo is just visible snaking under a cuff or into a collar. The men exchange apologetic glances with security. They were at school with some of them and back in the playground the future security guards had been at the top of the foodchain. No-one has forgotten this. The brighter boys, the ones who listened, the dull ones who worked, the ones whose parents came to the meetings, those, in short, whose teenage years were not bent on oblivion, they are at the top now. The others are doing life and putting a brave face on it.

Kate has pulled up at the kerb, watching taxis arrive, people coming and going. She clings to her story.The Palm House is a beacon in the dark night. *Well, if Billy cannot find that, he simply is not trying.* Meanwhile another part of her realises that the Palm House is no place for paedophiles these days. She releases the handbrake and squeezes her right foot onto the accelerator. *Six thirty.* Just over fourteen hours before she needs to come back. Soon the pink stone of the Anglican Cathedral looms before her, floodlit above its hidden roots. It begins well below street level in a one-time quarry, some time graveyard. As she turns into Hope Street, the Catholic Cathedral is visible too, a majestic tepi with some of her favourite stained glass. *Paddy's Wigwam.*

IT IS THE first hour of Sharon's evening shift and she is new to reception. She likes her job because she has to look nice. She is wearing her favourite high heels and when the manager comes past she can tell he is admiring her legs. No cleavage today. She has spent a lot of her second week's wages on nail extensions and this job gives her ample time in which to look at them. Long, square-tipped, with a pearly design, the manicurist called them very discreet. It is the old story. Sharon is waiting for life to begin when she meets a nice man and moves to... the Wirral, perhaps. Where better to do that than in this hotel? She has to deal with the guests, which she likes, *I'm a people person, me.* She also does the bills, which she does not like. Luckily Terry, the manager, likes to help Sharon. He would like to see a whole lot more of Sharon but he is married and Sharon is ambitious in her way. Terry is not on Sharon's radar except as a small daily boost to her ego. Seeing a large car parking outside she shifts in her high heels to get a better view. This is the kind of car which could drop her future husband under her nose and she adjusts her bra strap and her smile in anticipation. It is with disappointment then, that she sees a woman get out.

Married. Bloody typical! Hang on. She's driving. And it is with amazement that she realises the woman is alone. *In that car!* Sharon perks up. She is enterprising and not too proud to learn. *A four by four an'a new shearling. You could learn a few tricks here girl.* The woman who approaches the check-in desk looks tired. *Not a young woman, and why is she wearing those boots? They do nothing for her. She needs heels. Her hair's a disaster too.*The roots are showing a touch in Kate's blond hair; her skin is pale as papeand her eyes smudged with tiredness and this morning's make-up. *She is the delicate-looking kind some men go for.* Sharon prepares to take mental notes. *But I don't really do delicate. Me, I'm more the bubbly type.You want delicate. I'm stuffed.*

Kate pauses to let a couple exit and then takes over the heavy swing door and enters the lobby. She comes straight to the desk to check in. Sharon notices the nails. *Obviously.* Kate's nails are unpolished and neat; she wears a large diamond ring on her left hand and anonymous black trousers and jumper under the blonde coat. *Not a business client. What else can she be? I know. This is what rich people wear when they're not trying.* Sharon checks the booking. She is learning fast. *One person; one night. No man turning up then.Not on the pull either, by the look of her.* She likes the way Kate is unapologetic and polite. Clearly it has not crossed her mind to try and impress Sharon nor to confide in her. But on the other hand, unlike the local glamour wives who swan in here for dinner, she has no need to put her down either. Perhaps she is just used to it. Sharon writhes inwardly with pleasure as she contemplates a life staying in classy hotels. *Perhaps Mo's right and I could be a bit less picky.* Perhaps they don't need to be as handsome as all that.She practises an empty smile on Terry who smooches past to get to a screen.

'Business or pleasure?' asks Sharon with a winning smile and a hint of innuendo. She would say more but Terry is still lurking nearby. She would like a lot more information but cannot think of any legitimate reason to ask for it. There is flicker while they both register that Sharon's suit costs about the same as Kate's scarf. *Prada!*

Shit! Kate feels automatically guilty. But Sharon is thrilled and leans confidentially across the desk. This merits a porter. 'I'll get Angus.'

Angus is a boy of perhaps sixteen, dark hair, bad skin, big ideas. As he leads her along smartly pannelled corridors she reflects on what he would have been doing in her Liverpool of twenty years ago. *He'd have been one of those lads hanging around in the street and offering to 'mind yer car'.* Those unwise virgins who did not think their cars needed minding and certainly did not intend to pay for the privilege were rudely disabused. Often they found their cars stripped down overnight. In those days the dock road was a graveyard for the skeletons of cars whose owners had unwisely declined to pay for car-minding. Angus has a rolling walk, like his docker father, a twinkle in his eye and he pauses shamelessly for a tip as he leaves her room. Kate puts two pound coins in his hand and he winks at her as he closes the door behind him.*Yer never know. Nice lady. On 'er own.* This is what he says to Kev, the relief porter. Kev thinks Angus is pretty special.

A walk before dinner and Kate sees that Liverpool has fallen on better times and is glad. The Children's Hospital has made way for new building but Rodney Street, Hope Street, the Everyman Theatre, the cathedrals standing guard : they all look smarter than Kate remembers. Even the Phil, the Philharmonic Dining Rooms opposite the Philharmonic Concert Hall, looks more authentic, less of a self-parody than it used to. However, in a classic Liverpool gesture, one requiring very few fingers, the council has hit upon the idea of royal purple dustbins. They loiter in pairs outside the elegant Georgian facades, taking the piss. Liverpool never intends to get above itself. *Otty's Cafe is gone. Something trendy in its place. No-one says trendy any more.* In her room Kate checks her phone again. A text from Seb makes her smile. He is getting on well with Lisa's parents. *Is she going to be 'the one'? He's still quite young*. She plugs in her laptop and types in '*glass-house sefton park*'.

> *"Completed in 1896, the Palm House was a gift to the City by Henry Yates Thompson. It was designed by an Edinburgh firm, MacKenzie & Moncur who had branches in Glasgow and London. Their main works were in Balcarres Street, Edinburgh.*
> *The Palm House was designed in the tradition of Paxton's glass houses and was stocked originally with a magnificent collection of exotic plants. There were 9 marble statues on display inside together with a marble bench. On plinths around the outside there were a further 8 bronze/marble statues by Chavailiaud (1858-1921) of famous explorers and naturalists."*

Surely that should be 'Chavaillaud'? "Painted during the war to disguise it from the bombers, it fell into ruin during the period 1945 - 1986" - *just at the time I knew it* - "when a campaign was organised for its renovation." *Well they certainly did that. And now they hire it out for weddings et cetera. Hence the party tonight.*

In her bathroom Kate runs a deep bath with a liberal dose of tuber rose. The bathroom is faced in natural materials, scrubbed wood, limestone tiles, brass dishes for the candles. It has a fashionable, pared-down, middle-eastern feel as so many hotels do. She takes off her ring, a fifteenth wedding anniversary present from Rob, and puts it safely on the hand towel on the counter top beside the basin..*Could anything ever happen where a bath would not help?* Thinking now of the vulnerable presence within her, so much a part of her and yet another person in the making, she remembers having a bath in the hospital, in labour with

Sebastian and Max. Not tuber rose then, jasmine strong enough to blot out fear. Why hadn't she taken the Caesarian? *I wanted the real thing for me and for them. The mid-wife was impressed. Dear Malaika, what would I have done without her? Poor Rob. It took him longer to recover than me.*

'Bit of a design fault', chuckled the Registrar when he came by six hours later. Rob and the medic chuckled too. *Kick the tyres, why don't you?* Meanwhile the Handel, thoughtfully packed to welcome their infant sons as they took their first breath, played an endless theme tune to Kate's agony. To this day she winces when she hears the *Zadok The Priest.* Sinking into the hot water now, Kate inhales roses and closes her eyes, thinking of nine months' time. *This time we might skip the music and I shall beg respectfully for a Caesarian.* Drying herself on the giant white towels Kate catches sight of her naked body in the long mirror. The profile is not flattering but she puts her hand to her navel and feels a surge of love for her baby and even for herself.

SHALL I CALL her again? Don't know what to do now. I'll do the ring one, ring two, ring three.

IN BASILDON MARGARET and Sarah are on duty. So far it has been a quiet evening apart from a few snaps. Now the phone rings again and Sarah gets up.

'I'll go. Samaritans. Can I help you? ... No. Obviously not.'

'No-one there?'

'No. Another snap, Margaret. Can you put it in the log for me while I get the tea?' Tonight Billy is unlucky. No-one waits long enough for him to speak.

DINNER. CAN I face the dining room? Oh, why not? Kate pauses as she tucks the last towel around the fat chrome rail. Always tricky dressing for dinner alone but she has only brought one change of clothes, so tonight there's no problem. Kate goes down to dinner in a wrap-around black dress and the boots she came in. She eats dinner but her mind is already in the future. *In the park.* The understated brick of the walls is relieved by the Christmas decorations; seasonal table ornaments glint under the lights. *The food is meant to be good here. Park the car and walk down the small path to the glass house.* During the evening Kate is to walk down that path a dozen times. She looks through the menu. Her stomach churns.

Park the car and walk down the path.

'I'll have the scallops and the pasta, please.' *Park... don't speak. Wait til he's finished writing otherwise you won't get it. He'll forget.* 'A bottle of fizzy water. No ice. Oh and a glass of the Rioja.' *Park the...*'Thank you.' *Park the car and walk down the path.* The waiter brings her glass of wine. *...the path. Has he forgotten the water?*
They nod and smile as he puts it down. 'Can you bring me a bottle of fizzy water?' She cannot say 'no ice' again. It feels too fussy. *Park the car and walk down the path. Park the car and walk down the path.* The water arrives. A tall glass with ice cubes and lemon. The tear of the metal cap opening and the hiss of the gas before the water splashes onto the ice from a great height. The waiter turns out to be Angus again, demure this time, no winking. 'Thank you.'

Park the car... park the car... At last her mind forces itself out of the groove. *I could take a coffee and a croissant with me. Sit on the bench outside the Palm House.* Eating her first course the internal monologue of apprehension is still running. *Park the car. Sit on the bench. Enjoy the sunshine. See from there.*

'Is everything OK?'

'Fine thank you.' *I must sit where I can see.*

'Fish? Angus takes away her cutlery.'*Try to look as though I am on my way somewhere else.* More cutlery arrives. *Sit where I can see. Try to look...* Kate leans back politely to give him space to re-lay.*Try to look as if... Don't stop at the Palm House. Pass it and double back on myself. Must keep it in view*. The red wine leaves a film on the glass as she swills it around and admires the colour. *Park the car. Sit on the bench. Double back on myself. Keep it in view*.Looking round at the other guests between courses, she sees that the restaurant is busy now. *Keep it in view. Nothing in the park. No-one*.There is a wait for service. *Nothing in the park. No-one comes. Get back in the car and drive home. How shall I feel? A little foolish. Relieved. Thank you, Mother, I don't need your comments. Fuck off*. Her main course arrives. *Foolish. Relieved. Phone Rob from the car. Put my life back to normal.*

Winding pasta onto her fork, the story is different. *Park the car. Park the car. Park the car. Walk down the... Sit on the bench. See two little girls coming. See two little... how do I know they are... see two little... Approach them. Ask them. Try not to frighten them. Don't frighten them. Don't want people thinking I'm frightening them. Don't want people thinking it's me who's up to no good. Oh look, there goes Billy and the people think it's me............Don't want people thinking it's me... it's me... How would I explain... how would I... Are you Dorothy?*

As she feels the tagliatelle slippery in her mouth, a scent of truffle rich in her nose, she feels like congratulating herself on her good deed. She swallows with relief and the comforting sensation of food against the tongue, filling the soft palate, the feeling of a full mouth disappears until she again lifts her fork to her lips. *What would I... what...? Walk them as far as their school.* Kate pushes more food onto her fork.

Try not to look greedy. How old do I look? How do I look? Do I look pregnant? Do I look... that woman there, is she older than me? Is she older... is she, can't see, thinner?... Walk them as far as school. They are charming, holding my hands. My name's Kate. I was right to come. My name's Kate. I look over their shoulders in understanding at the teacher at the gate. I am modest. No, nothing at all, anyone would have... We are in silent understanding. We are the adults. Just like it was with Daddy. Marilyn shrivels like a witch when you throw water over her. But this time there is no-one at the school gates as she approaches with two little girls in tow and her imagination fails her. She puts down her knife and fork. *Now what? Go in? Speak to the teachers? The girls' parents?*

The waiter comes back with the pudding menu. *Do I look fat? Do I look... what have I eaten so far? chocolate ... lemon ... bread with the ... sorbet, why bother if you're only going to have a sorbet? ... do I look ... Decide for God's sake... the boy will think you... decide now...* She orders the lemon tart and remembers to drink the water in front of her. The last thing she needs tomorrow is a hangover. The ice has melted. Her fingers curl and uncurl around the wet glass. *Must do my nails. I can see him now. That's him, lumbering in old clothes towards the glass house. Must be him. Not the girls. Can't see the girls. What if I meet Billy?* As she opens her mouth to order an espresso he has seen her too. *A beautiful recognition between us. Bound to be. I'm the only one to understand him. Daddy had a special... he would be proud... a lot of people wouldn'....* Kate waits for her coffee. *Sitting on the bench with Billy. Billy confiding yet more. I have saved him from tragedy. Billy sweet and grateful. I am vindicated.* Kate extracts a tip for the waiter and puts it on the white cloth. In her head, the picture has changed again.

Billy sweet and approaching with a knife... path, a large figure is approaching, ... the wind... child in a red coat ... in a hurry, eyes fixed... no kindness ... hurried along... stumbles clipped on the side of the head... catch ... wind ... whips away. The child ... shrinks ...words scour her heart ... conveyed along at speed ... She dives into the lift - *serves me right* - and escapes into the present whilst all the possibilities of tomorrow continue to run alongside one another in her head.

ALONG AN INTERNAL path, a large figure is approaching, bundled up against the wind. A child in a red coat skips to keep up. The large figure is in a hurry, eyes fixed ahead. There is no kindness in the way the child is hurried along. The child stumbles and is clipped on the side of the head for clumsiness. The distance is too great to catch the words which the wind's discretion whips away. The child however shrinks visibly as the words scour his heart and he is conveyed along at speed by an unyielding grip on the wrist.

Wednesday morning 0633

IN LARK LANE Uma is opening the shop in the dark. She is only just in time. Her younger brother, Krishna, arrives within minutes to sort the newspapers which lie in great bundles by the front door; it is Uma's job to haul them inside and it is not her place to keep him waiting. He comes straight from his prayers, taking himself very seriously since their father died. He stopped all the same for a bacon sandwich on the way. If she is wise, she will not comment. Patrick the paper boy arrives at the last minute to deliver the newspapers before rushing late into school. A cigarette and a Mars bar are his breakfast. He does not believe in prayers and he does not acknowledge Uma. Her beauty and her foreignness frighten him. So do his feelings for her.

KATE WAKES EARLY in Hope Street. She switches on Radio Four. Thought for the Day. But it is not the thought from the radio which takes her. It is the memory of Sunday morning a few weeks ago when she and Rob made love. This must be when Leila was conceived according to her dates. They are having an especially tender moment. Kate looks at Rob this morning as he sits on the bed with his back to her. He is getting up to let the dogs out, make the tea and come back to bed. His hair is as yet untamed by the morning routine and at the nape of his neck and around his ears, the thick, dark hair is greying. Her love for him is awakened, wells up and translates itself into action. She reaches out to stroke his shoulder.

'Come back soon. There is a soft fullness between her legs that she would like to share with him.' He smiles at her and she can tell he really sees her as she does him. There they both are, middle-aged now in the morning light, yet the room is full of love and excitement, full of tenderness. When he comes back he sits on her side of the bed and they drink their tea and chat. When the tea is gone, so are the words. He holds her hand and she takes it to her cheek as she looks into his eyes. He can see the unevenness of her skin, the spider's web of tiny creases between her collar bones and her breasts where she has lain asleep on the sheets. He feels his love for her more deeply than usual. This morning it is not the shadow of the pretty girl he met in the flat above the Tuileries that attracts him, although even today he catches a glimpse of her as she brushes her hair or crosses her legs or stalks upstairs in high heels - a rare treat. This morning it is the here and now Kate, mother of twins, forty-five, unbrushed, unwashed and luscious that is awakening his body, his soul. Her skin is soft and fine and creased like an old cloth, nearly transparent. Her smell familiar yet exciting, he wants to bury his face in her neck. But he waits. *What will she want? How to extend the moment?*

As he takes his hand from her cheek she catches his wrist and brings his thumb to her mouth. She is still looking him in the eye as she takes his thumb a little at a time between her teeth and swishes her tongue around it. For Rob the feeling transfers itself straight to his balls and to his delight his penis springs into life. Is it her tongue or the invitation in her eyes that is so exciting? He gazes at his wife in admiration and runs his right hand down her thigh past the silk hem and lets it linger around the knee. Kate releases his thumb from the gentle grip of her teeth and locks her lips around it, sucking hard. His hand explores her inner thigh. For a moment or so they sit entranced with each other and then with a wriggle of her hips, Kate has spread her legs wide and now she lies flat throwing the pillow that was in the way across the room. The dark aubergine silk of her short nightdress is beautiful across her pale skin; the curve of her breast beneath the silk as she breathes hard is irresistible. As he climbs onto the bed on all fours and kneels above her, she pushes him back to sit on his heels. He watches her and waits as she slowly catches hold of the silk hem of her nightdress and comes closer to stroke him through it. The little shoulder straps have falled around her arms and her breasts are emerging from the silk which feels wonderful against her nipples.

Now Rob has to close his eyes and open his mouth as his head falls back with the intensity of the sensation.The noise he makes as she barely touches him through the silk excites her still more. She curls up on the duvet beside him, her breast against his thigh, her head in his groin and lets her tongue explore what the silk so recently disguised. Now she is lying on her front as his tongue and rough chin tickle the back of her neck and then all the way down her spine. The weight of him reassuring and exciting falls on the back of her thighs as he works tantalisingly up and down her back with his fingertips, his tongue. She cannot move and loves it. They are naked now and she can feel the fuzzy hair and the warmth of his chest in the small of her back as his hands creep underneath her body to pinch her nipples. One hand holds her down by one wrist spread on the sheet above her head. His breath is hot in her ear and he explores the lobe with his teeth. Now one of her hands is between her legs but he wrenches it away and enters her from behind with a cry.

For Kate the simultaneous sensations of exquisite pleasure and the pain as he stretches her inside, the roughness of his movements, the charge of his excitement, are too much and she arches her back and shouts as the ecstasy overtakes her. Now she buries her face in the sheet as he too falls from the great height of his pleasure and he lowers himself gently to lie on her. I am going - isn't that what the Japanese say? He turns her head to cover her mouth with his and as they lie together she can feel the wetness of their bodies mingling between them. The wet softness of him still rocking slightly against her buttocks is indistinguishable from his tongue as it explores inside her lips, the touch of his fingers as he plays with her hair. His eyes are open and as beautiful as the night sky. *I can touch the space between the stars.*

NOW KATE NEEDS some tea. She finds it hard to use room service. A reluctance to be waited on, to ask for things and have people meet her needs and a natural shyness on the telephone all contribute. Eventually she overcomes these reservations and uses the telephone by her bed. *Order some tea. You can scarcely fetch it yourself. Seven o'clock and still dark.* A sense of secrecy, of the illicit accompany this drinking of tea off a beautifully laid tray with the street lights still on outside. *No time for meditation.* A small bowl of honey comes with the tea. She dips her finger in it and licks it clean. *Rob.* Her body aches for him.

From her window she can see Falkner Street where she briefly lived years ago. *A wonderful Georgian house. Only cold water but the rats on the stairs were mostly dead.* In the basement was an enormous kitchen the size of the house's footprint. Kate tried to clean it and put it back into service. The ghosts of the servants who had worked there looked on as she scrubbed the floor and lit the old gas cooker. They knew she was only playing. This kitchen must have served a family of ten and their staff. What dishes had been created here to be eaten upstairs. The moulds and silver trays, the hair sieves and isinglass have long since disappeared from the open shelves. The atmosphere remains but this is not a place to cook for yourself and soon Kate gives up and goes back to eating at the Union and the wine bars on Mount Pleasant.

Standing by the window with her tea, Kate remembers all of a sudden a trip she made from Falkner Street. Alastair rolling up in his Fiat, all of them piling in. Pete Walker was there. Fiona. JP. *That's right it was the beach. Southport beach.* They were going to the beach for a barbecue at night. *My final year. June '79. There was something strange. What was it? Something odd happened.* Something haunts her. Her mind stretches as far back into that afternoon as it can. *The weather was not great, a lot of wind. Day trippers going home, children. A minibus full of children, handicapped children.*

The minibus had been waiting in the car park as they drew up. *The door was open* - they were waiting for the stragglers before they could go. *No-one else seemed to notice.*

Alastair and JP are unpacking the car, then Pete is running onto the beach to find stones to build a fire. Kate sits in the car for a long moment looking out of the window. She was going out with Pete until recently. *I shouldn't have come.* A large figure is approaching, bundled up against the wind. A child in a red coat skips to keep up. The large figure is in a hurry, eyes fixed ahead. There is no kindness in the way the child is hurried along. The child stumbles and is clipped on the side of the head. The child is crying. He is conveyed along at speed by an unyielding grip on the wrist.

'Come on Kate! Give us a hand!' And at last the poor, little creature with a terrible deformity in his face, now visible under the hood of his red coat, struggles into the minibus. The sliding door shuts and the bus pulls away. 'Kate!'

'Coming!'

EIGHT

KATE FEELS CLOSE to danger. Instinctively she puts her cup down on the window ledge and pulls the hotel robe closer around her. Trying to ease her mind, she looks again out of her hotel window and takes in the familiar draw of the water, the irresistible sea-side light which illuminates the streets in all weathers. Liverpool's charm lies in its promise of travel, of distant shores and visiting exotics. She once sat on the steps of what they called 'the bombed-out church', actually St Luke's, with an Egyptian tramp. *Back then we called them tramps.* His story had captivated her. Liverpool had then, and retains now, the promise of a jumping-off point which is not just about being where the land meets the sea. Egypt at that time was of unimagined strangeness, a place in her father's tiny, black and white photos. There was Brian in a pith helmet. Other ranks sat nearby on the sand attended by two small Arab boys and some goats. On the back in Brian's careful writing 'Self, Smith, Barnes, Timpson. Before the show'. It was years before Kate realised what show he meant.

Liverpool. A place to embark for yet stranger realms, distant continents. But that is not all. Not only a port but a bridge between the everyday and the magical, between the self she knows and her true self, the hidden self which lies in waiting and which she is slowly uncovering. *Well. I've done it now. Chucked in the rules and all the support that goes with them. This is my last chance to turn back. I could see the city and drive home. No-one would ever know. All that is on the record is one snap.* But she does not turn back. She can taste again the recklessness of youth. She can sense the real self and its power, so deeply hidden beneath the veils of biddable wife and circumspect mother.

SHOULD I CHECK out now or later? Now is better. Pay my bill. Throw my stuff in the car. Never know what may happen... don't want to have to come back to get things. May not be time. Just the mascara. Boiled egg not a good look. That'll do. Don't want to look as though.... Christ, no. Trousers. Jumper. Coat and boots. That's fine. Oh God I'm nervous. What the hell am I doing? Nobody knows where I am. Can't call anyone; they'll want an explanation. Tell the hotel. Perhaps I should leave my stuff after all. I know, I'll leave my luggage by the desk. That way, if I don't come back, someone will notice. Eventually. But she did not leave her bag. It was neater in the end to throw it on the back seat, cover her tracks and go. At least, this was her plan. *Just me and you, then, baby. We'll be OK. A brief walk in the park. I'm sure he won't be there and then we'll drive home. At least I'll have cleared my conscience. Come on, Kate. Don't make a meal out of this.* Kate hears again her mother's voice within. *'Storm in a teacup', 'mountain out of a mole-hill'* - Marilyn was never short of a cliche and all of them impressed upon Kate that her feelings were out of place, excessive, self-indulgent. *Hi Daddy. Hello, chick. How are you?Not so good. Can't phone him either. Bloody hell, Edward. Eight o'clock and my things are packed up again. Send Rob a text, 'looking fwd to tonight'. I really am. I will be so glad to see him.*

Call the lift. Feeling like a good wife - is this somehow absolving her from the deceit of what she is about to do? *God, I'm not having an affair after all.* She pushes away a question about Rob's feelings and punches the button for 'Ground Floor'. The lift arrives at reception where the desk is awash with Christmas cheer. She pays the bill and tips Sharon.

'Great room, thanks.'

'No problem, Madam.' Her diamond ring still lies on the hand towel upstairs. She tosses her bag into the car and slams the driver's door.

IT IS A matter of ten minutes to Sefton Park from here even with what passes for rush-hour traffic. Too soon she is parked just a moment's walk from the Palm House and decides to wait ten minutes or so before leaving the car. She did not bring coffee after all. As she sits and waits she sees again Sefton Park under heavy snow. The Winter sunset is violet through the trees and the broken panes of the glass house have an eerie quality in the strange light. Colours from the sky reflect back off the snow. The whole scene is from a Bonnard.

Eight thirty and, clutching her mobile, Kate strides down the tarmac path from the road to the Palm House. *They have not stinted on the restoration. McKenzie and Moncur would be proud.* There is no-one about and Kate glances discreetly to left and right as she walks. No school-children walk this way and, she now realises, it is much too far away from Lark Lane to be on the way to the school she had in mind. It is a short walk and yet her boots are giving her a blister and after a couple of turns around the glass building, she finds a bench to sit on. She feels ridiculous, conspicuous, stood up. She hates waiting.

SHE IS IN the Cafe de la Paix and Rob is late because he is in bed with a tall Parisian with green, oval eyes and red hair. Kate has just called him from the payphone near the lavatories, 'vous desirez un jeton, mademoiselle?' *His voice was strange. He was not alone.* Kate thinks of Valmont writing his billets doux to one as he makes love to another. Rob says he has been delayed and tells her to wait. *But I know where he is.* Part of her that acknowledges that the man she is in love with is betraying her and every one who passes can tell. The betrayal is in the single glass on the table, in the way she has not taken her coat off, in the way the waiters avoid her, in the way she does not look at her watch, the cigarette ends in the ashtray. *Twenty to.* She waits for Billy just as she did for Rob. The weather is much colder than yesterday and the bench is icy. She begins to pace again and then sits down as the raw flesh of her heel touches the inside of her boot. Movement catches her eye to the right.

ALONG AN INTERNAL path, a large figure is approaching, bundled up against the wind. A child in a red coat skips to keep up. The large figure is in a hurry, eyes fixed ahead. There is no kindness in the way the child is hurried along. The child stumbles. *That's how my mother was towing me along when I fell and cut my lip. I had a red coat like that.* Kate fingers the scar on her bottom lip. She is on her feet now, her whole body straining towards recognition, above all, to decide whether the adult figure is male or female. Her eyes run in the wind. She knows her nose is scarlet. The figures proceed purposefully towards the glass-house and as they come in range Kate opens her mouth to call. Billy! Dorothy! It is like a story heard in childhood come to life.

Here they are! The figures from her imagination. *And yet......* And yet she does not call out. She cannot be sure and she already feels ridiculous. They pass within feet of her and swoop off onto another path. As they go Kate recognises a female attitude in the adult's walk and hears the child call her 'Nan'. The lone word reaches her ear above the drone of a police helicopter which is suddenly above them. Are they looking for Billy? Relief and disappointment flood through her but she does not move. She looks down and sees her empty finger. Her ring is missing. Her energy leaves her. Her mobile has no reception so she must wait. She is not the good wife now.

'What happens, Mummy, to bad people that the police do not catch?'

'They are always caught in the end, Kathryn. Never fear. Always caught in the end.' As Marilyn is afraid she will be.

Wednesday morning 0845

MY BIRTHDAY. HAPPY Birthday dear Billy, Happy Birthday to you. No-one sings to Billy. No-one sings to Billy when he's been naughty. 'You've been naughty again, Billy!' I wish Maeve was here. It's not her day. 'You an' your fuckin' birthday, Billy!'. That's what Sheila says.

TEN TO NINE. Only a solitary jogger has passed her. *Starting to sleet.* Again she stares at her phone. *No reception.* The park is not how she remembers. In her imagination a place of short walks, Autumn leaves and a little-known hide-away in the glass house. In reality this has turned into an overwhelmingly large expanse of park with a well-advertised and well-frequented Palm House. *A place manifestly unsuited to the seduction of children.*

Wednesday morning 0930

VIV SCURRIES UP the road protecting her hair against the weather with her hands. Her first client is due now. *Another perm at half price.* She cannot afford to let them down, the OAPs. They are her daily bread. *Where are the young people?* That's what Viv needs. *Girls with a bit of get-up-and-go about them.* A bit of ambition such as she had at their age. She looks across at Fat Sheena with fondness and despair. She took her on to help Sheena's mother, one of Viv's friends from the old days. Where else was Sheena going to find a job? But still Viv longed for an assistant with flair, with a future. *'Yer've a mouth like the Mersey Tunnel, 'Gerroff that phone gerl! Worrava told yer?' she yells, twisting rollers into another shampoo and set. 'Mind the hearing aid, Viv!'* The bell on the door jangles as another old lady steps cautiously out of the shop - *salon, Sheena, we call it a salon!* - back into the world, like a neatly trimmed radish, face red from the dryer, white hair crimped on top. *Bless them.* Viv feels sentimental all of a sudden and by the time she is putting the kettle on she feels her big-hearted self. *What would they do without me? We keep each other going. And then there's always Elsie to look forward to. And one day I'll get Uma in here.*

AT HALF PAST nine Kate is freezing but no wiser. The helicopter has skirted the trees and disappeared again. Out of ideas she walks back to the car and calls Billy's number. But the signal is still not strong enough and she hears the three beeps of a failed call. She does not know what to do. Fear and a sense of futility are contending in her stomach. She feels heavy and stupid. An idea surfaces, suppressing these unpleasant feelings. *I'll drive over to the school, to Lark Lane. Just have a nose about.*

THE IRISH LOVER once lived here and this in itself makes Kate feel better. She remembers his room, dark even in Summer, his house-mate across the hall and the way he turned his beautiful Persian girlfriend's picture to the wall that afternoon. Patrick read his poetry to her. Patrick made her mint tea which burnt her lips with fresh mint and sugar crystallising on the edge of the glass. Nearly thirty years later the guilt and excitement, the enchantment of that afternoon are almost tangible. She was engaged to someone else at the time. Kate catches sight of her guilty hands. *Oh my God, my ring!*

HERE SHE IS at the divide in the road which leads away from the park to Lark Lane and things look different. She dials the hotel number and tells Sharon she has forgotten her ring.

'Has someone found it?'

'I'll just check.' There is a long pause whilst Sharon and Angus admire the diamond at this moment on Sharon's own finger. It is a wrench, but she clears her throat and replies. 'Yes, Mrs Hurst. I have it safe and sound for you.' *Thank God.*

Kate leaves the car outside a newsagent's and walks the length of the small parade of shops. The year of the Royal Wedding 1981, Kate brought Rob to see Liverpool, visit old friends. They found the city riven by riot as the rest of the country succumbed to Diana fever. The Somali Club was burnt down. Grove Street and Mount Street glowed with embers of political hatred and the flames of free-lance arsonists. But the riots did not to Lark Lane. Then came the official Heseltine regeneration : Liverpool as theme park, a parody of itself. Liverpudlians, like Venetians, are always playing themselves. Lark Lane once a peaceful backwater has become rather chic. *The kind of place Max would live. Viv's the hairdresser - surely I remember that? That was there.*

Inside the widows and spinsters of the parish form a short row under the dryers. They are a naturally talkative bunch but deaf and under the dryers they resort to magazines and staring into space. Just one old soul is refusing to go quietly into old age; the unwavering cauliflower perm is not for Elsie. Viv herself is pasting on the deep purple mix that will restore to Elsie's head a firy imitation of the red hair she sported as a young woman. *Not the kind of job you could leave to Fat Sheena.* As a girl Elsie had sung with a band around the dance halls of the North West. Until she married Norman, men had thrown themselves at her feet from Manchester to Wigan. Even as a married woman, mother, mother-in-law and now widow, Elsie had preserved something of the glamorous mystique she had cultivated when she was performing. Norman had worshipped her and Elsie was kind to him right until the end. They were very happy. Since Norman passed on Elsie has always kept a man around her. *One of my young men,* she calls them.

Viv herself is glamorous in a way. At fifty her decollete is as deep as a railway cutting. It sets off her tan and her jewellery. Her blond hair is freshly lacquered and she clicks on her kitten-heeled mules from one old girl to the next with a Marilyn Monroe wiggle. 'Keep young and beautiful' is Viv's motto, and she'll sing it too at the drop of a hat. Bending theatrically behind each customer to talk to her in the mirror gives Viv the excuse to peek a hundred times a day at her own reflection, to adjust her hair or admire her earrings. 'You are a case, Viv.' They love her. *Never wanted to do anything else and then after Keith left, I never had the chance. You don't with four kids, do you?*

NEXT DOOR AN off-licence has security grilles such as Kate associates with banks and benefit offices and other places where desperation leads to violence. The shopfront declares its name to be *Firewater* but its clientele know it unashamedly as 'the Paki shop'. Sure enough, behind the counter and a metal grille, a tee-total Pakistani gentleman sits counting takings. The narcotics forbidden to him by his religion are cheerfully sold to the Christians. Father Michael comes by for a half of Irish whiskey from time to time, a sight which Habib finds a deeper mystery than Christianity itself. His predecessor came in his cassock. Father Michael is more jeans and leather jackets. Next door the infidel Uma minds the newsagents in an immaculate sari, a small diamond in her nose, a *bindhi* marking her third eye. She smiles shyly at Viv's jokes when Viv comes to buy cigarettes. Uma shares them with her friends at the temple, holding her sari in front of her mouth as she blasphemes. Not against God, she would never do that, but against the men who fashion her life. Men always come off worst in Viv's jokes - so different from Uma's real life. Viv is like a bird of paradise to Uma. Viv would like to do her hair. The heavy black plait hangs tantalisingly down her back.

'Come into the salon one day, Uma. Go on, I won't charge you. Let me and Sheena give you a make-over. You won't know yourself.' Uma thinks it would be fun to spend time with Viv and Sheena who is shy like her, but she does not want to be made over. She likes her plait and her sari. She likes to look on from the sidelines. It is just female company she misses. Her mother has been dead some time.

KATE PATROLS THE parade again staring this time at the houses opposite. *The school has gone, or am I in the wrong place? The church is there.* The stubble is almost blue against his white skin and, inexperienced as she is, when he parts her lips and enters her she realises he is huge. He sat cross-legged on the bed like a yogi and showed her how to sit upon him so that they could rock back and forth. His arms wrapped around her, her legs around him, his mouth covered her eyes with kisses while her fingers stroked his hair and the back of his neck. She wanted to die like that. *Wow, Patrick.* Absolute bliss. Kate feels the shudder even today. But each of them belonged to someone else and their paths did not cross again. Those few encounters haunt her as she stands so near to his front door. Green curtains hang at the bedroom window now. This part of her past she has never shared with Rob.

At last Kate ventures in to the hairdressers and is confronted with six pairs of interested eyes. The eponymous Viv tears herself from the mirror, brush in hand, and confirms what Kate already knows. *The school went, oh, ten years ago.* Viv is mortified. She thought she had a paying customer. *Nice hair too, nice face. I could've done something with her. She doesn't do much with herself.*

'Was it something I said?' Viv makes them laugh as the door shuts behind Kate. Kate hears the cracked laughter which greets all Viv's banter, a ribald commentary on life as it proceeds. She smiles back at them through the glass dor, anxious to be included in the laughter, offering to be one of them after all, though she cannot stay. She feels rejected, an outsider. *And where am I not an outsider? Why have I chosen this?* Her hands hold her stomach under her coat. With her children, she belongs. Back in the car, her options are running out.

BILLY IS WATCHING television. Sheila is in her office, a powerful woman with short hair and a harrowed face which her heavy make-up fails to disguise . Her once chestnut hair is now salt and pepper, her neck too wide for a woman. Her clothes too are mannish. A check shirt with the sleeves rolled up, bottle green trousers with socks and flat shoes, a knitted, navy waistcoat. And yet there is nail varnish and her gold jewellery sits uneasily on arthritic joints. A bunch of keys, her emblem of office, hangs from her plastic belt. Sheila keeps West Highland terriers and a caravan on the East coast. Her terriers win prizes. She prefers animals to people. All is quiet. *Grab a fag an' a coffee before the next fuckin' emergency.* But no. Sheila's mobile is ringing in her waistcoat pocket. A number she does not know.

'Hello?'

'Hello?' The voice is female, uncertain. *Posh.* Fortuitously Maeve comes in and hovers nervously. Sheila is about to enjoy herself and waves Maeve to a plastic chair against the wall. She likes an audience. Maeve crumples into it. Her head is bent over her cup so that her little blond perm sits above her beige clothes and her face is absent. You would never know how strong Maeve is to look at her. Her shoes fasten with velcro.

'Have I got the right number for Billy?'

'Billy!' Outrage contends with black humour in Sheila's throaty voice, the most attractive thing about her. She speaks with exaggerated politeness, winking at Maeve to signal an opportunity for Maeve to admire her cleverness. *Keep up, Maeve. Where's me audience? D'you think I keep you on for your health?* 'Billy, now Billy Who would that be?' Sheila rolls the name around her mouth speculatively.

Kate's voice is not in her favour and she knows it. Middle class, apologetic. Sheila can spot a middle-class bitch at a hundred paces and she soon gets shot of ladies who would like to improve her regime. Prison visitors, social workers, probation officers, voluntary workers of all persuasions. *I've met 'em all. Voluntary work, my arse - too much money! Dropping in when they feel like it! What fuckin' use are people like that?* Their idealistic views take no account of the daily reality she has to deal with. *It's all human rights now. Human fuckin' rights! I'm sorry! What do they know about it?* Opportunities, according to Sheila, foisted upon people so unpredictable and violent, so unfathomable, (the words she uses are more emotive) that the courts have passed them over to her. *Their families have banged them up here for the rest of their natural. What I do with'em, that's my business, thank you very much.* Three meals a day, their own TV and a dedicated phone line to the Samaritans, that is as far as Sheila is prepared to go. It is as far as Sheila can afford to go.

Park House is a private unit, dependent upon the good will of the council who pay the charges and as far as they are concerned she is doing the trick. It developed from an old people's home; indeed some of the old people still quake on the ground floor when they hear the 'secure' population above them. Sheila's unit allows the authorities to remove from the hospital or prison population some of the nastiest and most problematic characters in their care - and at a bargain price. They are not inclined to ask many questions. She sank everything into the business after the divorce.

Moved her in with us before leaving me. Can you believe it? Brought her home with him. Comes 'ome from the pub one night. Remember Norma? he says, large as life. She an' Chris have split up. I said she could kip 'ere til she gets 'erself sorted. Oh did you, I says, but I was green as grass. And I loved 'im. A month later they were setting up fuckin' home him an' Chris.

They only stayed until they had saved the deposit for the rent. Sheila had an abortion when he left. *Enough bastards in the world already.* She still lives as if under siege. Surrounded by the disaffected and the violent, she saves her feelings for her girls, the bevy of small dogs who wait at home. The world was out to get her.*The VAT people, Health and Safety, you name it.* But she could stick up for herself. *I'm not about to be bullied into anything by some little tart on the phone.* Not at this late stage. *I knew her type. Ringing, checking up. They don't want to do the job themselves, just poking their noses in and making life even more fuckin' difficult.* This one clearly had no official capacity or she would have said so by now. Sheila lights a small cigarette and draws heavily on the filter. Then she throws her feet up on the desk and leans back for the cabaret.

Rashly Kate cannot help but explain.

'Yes, I am sorry to bother you, but he rang me from this number yesterday and I needed to speak to him again. Is he there?'

'Is he here! I'll say he's here. Where else would he be? Down the chip shop? This is a secure hospital, love, not the bleedin' Adelphi! Who are you?' Sheila exchanges knowing glances with her assistant Maeve and presses 'speakerphone' so that they can relish this caller together. Maeve could not sit after all. She is leaning against the filing cabinet, mug in hand, trying to look as though she is enjoying the show. But Maeve has her worries. *He hasn't complained, has he? I'll kill'im.* She can feel the violence rising in her thighs. She squeezes the burning hot mug in her palm. Anything to stop the anger coming out.

'Just a friend, actually.'

'Oh aye? He hasn't been out of this ward for fifteen years. He doesn't have friends. Who are you? *Actually?*' Idly Sheila checks her teeth for lipstick in a desk-top mirror as she speaks. On the 'actually' she raises her eyes to smile at Maeve and make sure she gets the full value of the repartee.

'I, um...' *Don't mention the Samaritans.* 'I...Well, I....The thing is I heard it was his birthday and...'

'I'll give him birthday. He thinks every day's his fucking birthday! Are you his new social worker? One of the bizzies?'

'No. I...'

'Do you want to visit him then? Nip round for a cuppa tea?'

'Um, no. '

'What, don't yer fancy a nice piece'a cake with our Billy. I'll get the silver out.'

'No, um, actually. The thing is...'

'No, '*um, actually*', I thought not.' Maeve knows what is good for her and smiles sycophantically. Without Sheila she would have no job. If it hadn't been for Sheila tidying up her record, as she put it, she could have been out of work for life after last time. 'Well, I mean, we're only human, aren't we? Can't help losing our temper now and again, can we?' asked Sheila at the interview. In fact Sheila has taken a liking to Maeve. *Likes dogs too. Bit heavy handed with people, but I can keep an eye on her.*

'Well, I don't know who you are or what you want '*actually*' '- the sarcasm is heavy-handed but stings all the same - 'but steer clear of friend Billy, love. I say who Billy sees, '*actually*', and when, and if I were you I'd change your number if Billy's got it. The little toe-rag won't be using my phone again. On a good day he's not dangerous but he don't have so many good days if you get my meanin'. And nor do I. Now geroff the line before I find out who you really are.' Sheila puts down the phone and sucks hard on the triumphant cigarette before stubbing it out in the saucer on her desk. Maeve looks on in awe.

'Now then, Nurse Highsmith, look sharp!' she says with a mock severity which thrills Maeve.

REACHING HER CAR is a struggle. Her emotions, at war with each other, reveal to Kate the full extent of her self-interest in this adventure. She had wanted to vindicate herself, her own ideas. *I wanted to show Andy how I was right, how superior to all the Samaritans' rules.* Now the utter humiliation of being wrong, the sharp words of the matron at the home, send shooting pains through her mind and her stomach gripes in sympathy. Liverpool is not such a friendly place now. And she still has to get her ring. The worst of it is, she has let Billy down. She has put herself first although she had convinced herself otherwise until this moment. And yet there is relief too, Dorothy is beyond her help, safe in her own way. In the driving seat there is a collapse, a further loss of energy and Kate realises it is fifteen hours since she ate. Yet she is not hungry. This morning's coffee and adrenalin have held her up until now but she remembers Leila. Slowly she unstops the bottle of water she took from her hotel room and drinks it dry. Then with a sigh, she takes off her coat, throws it awkwardly on the back seat and turns the key. The car noses out of the parking space and into the road. The park road is only intermittently busy and just now hers is the only car about. Her mouth is dry and her heart still beating fast. Sheila's words linger. *She had my number. If I can get my ring back I can forget this whole escapade. I need never tell anyone.*

Up Penny Lane, she is doing barely thirty but as she approaches a zebra crossing a small child runs across. The mother, watching helpless on the pavement with a pushchair and another toddler, opens her mouth to scream. Kate hits the brakes and continues to move forward in slow motion towards the child who is laughing over his shoulder towards his mother, daring her to chase him. The car stops short of the crossing and in any case the boy is now on the opposite pavement. Kate automatically winds down her window to commiserate with the mother - she should have been holding onto that child but Kate knows too well how easy it is to give up that particular struggle with boys. The young woman in the purple puffa and the ponytail wears the extreme thinness of poverty and perhaps addiciton. She throws down her cigarette in order to raise one apologetic hand at Kate. Then she and the pushchair stalk across the crossing, the girl stooping slightly to give the toddler the benefit of her frustration, her resentment and fear in the form of a slap around the head.

Turning left at the top of Penny Lane where the fishmonger's used to be Kate realises she is in shock. Her body is shaking so much she has to pull over and sit for a while. Eventually she feels able to continue and soon she is drawing up once more outside the hotel. Sharon reluctantly returns the diamond and Kate with a gasp of relief gets back behind the wheel and heads out of town towards the M62. She feels much less guilty with the ring on her finger. *Four hours it took me to get up here. Should be home late afternoon and Rob'll be there.* Rob's car is waiting for him at the airport. *His flight arrives at two.*

Wednesday morning 1148

Kate drives slowly now and with extra care, as if she were carrying a delicate passenger or a trifle on the front seat beside her. As a child she lay with her head on his lap as her father drove. The bench seat of the old Morris had no seat belts but they travelled secure in a mutual trust and adoration that made them immortal. She will never know that feeling of total safety again despite all her efforts to recreate it in her adult life. *Despite all my manipulations.* Kate is aware that she is not herself, that she has lost all confidence in her own judgment. Suddenly the familiar controls of the car, the automatic responses to speed and distance, are no longer familiar or automatic. She has to think about driving and at each moment she is aware of her power to destroy herself and others in such a way that each uneventful mile becomes a miraculous surprise to her.

The journey takes longer at sixty than at her usual eighty, but when she stops half way to get petrol and eat some fruit and breakfast cereal, she is doing well. *No roadworks Southbound. Should be home by half four.* By half past three, however, she is behind schedule. On the M40 a dangerous mist comes and goes with the rise and fall of the land. The bruised sky threatens snow, hastening the Winter dusk. Visibility is poor. The homewardbound traffic is both weary and in a hurry. Yet everything keeps moving without regard for the light, the weather or the resources of the short-tempered drivers. A fatal combination.

Wednesday afternoon 1630

It is not until the A34 that there is a serious delay. She is perhaps half an hour from home when she sees the tail lights across both lanes of stationary traffic, some flashing to warn the next-comers. The mist has cleared here and sun is setting ahead of her; the sky takes on a brief pink glow and the faint shadows of the trees explore the edges of the fields. They are nearing the shortest day. On seeing the lights ahead Kate is relieved to observe her reflexes kick in. *Right foot off the accelerator - second nature - and then the slow squeeze of the brake.* She falls into line behind the car in the outside lane and switches on the news. There is nothing new, only the usual round of broken promises, misunderstandings and injustices that people never tire of hearing. The cadences of interviewer and victim - aggressive and defensive respectively - are instantly recognisable. Kate puts on some Mahler instead and then, rejecting that too, resolves to sit in silence as the traffic inches forward and it grows dark around her. She notices that there are no cars coming the other way. A wrenching in her guts anticipates the worst - a pile-up involving both carriageways. The 'carnage' of which the radio is so fond -

man reduced to meat. *Road pizza, as the boys glibly call it.* Kate shivers. *Do I have a temperature?*

WHEN SHE WAS little Kate had suffered the usual afflictions of her generation - mumps, chicken pox, measles, German measles and the odd bout of flu. A temperature was inevitably the first sign. *I used to like it.* These temporary, mild inconveniences brought out the best in Marilyn who would have liked to have been a nurse. For Kate they meant a day or two in bed, extra comics. *Time off from doing my best. I could allow Mummy to take care of me without loss of face.* Houses were cold in a penetrating way in England before the advent of central heating. Accordingly, on those days, Kate was confined to bed until after lunch so that the gas poker could coax the sitting room fire into life and it was warm enough for an invalid to sit on the sofa wrapped in a blanket. Even as she senses the flannelette sheets of her childhood against her skin, at some other level Kate is endlessly replaying the scene in the park. She is berating herself for her pride, her gullibility. Now, in this moment, she must face with especial clarity, that she has blown it this time - she has made a fool of herself. There is no way she can reframe what she has done so that it seems to her honourable, let alone commendable. *How to face Rob? I have to tell him.* It does not occur to her that he might react with compassion to her internal ordeal, with understanding to her dilemma. Years of married kindness and mutual support have not shifted Kate's expectation of judgment, a judgment that begins within.

Wednesday afternoon 1700

IT IS DARK now. They have been waiting for half an hour, uncomfortable, trapped in a traffic jam, before the accident is in sight. The ins and outs of lane-changing and jostling for imaginary gains give way, in Kate's case, to horror. Others slow down out of curiosity. Meanwhile her limbs turn to water as she sees the extent of the damage.

OUTSIDE IT'S ICY and dark. An accident on the drive home from school. I clutch my satchel to me in the back of the Ford Popular. Red cloth seats under my fingers. Bodies propped like dummies against the wall over the railway bridge. Horror coming from Mother in front. Too terrified to feel at all for me. Iron entered my soul that night. You can see it in the photos.

IT HAS GROWN dark around her and the flashing yellow lights of heavy equipment and the blue lights of police and fire service vehicles deprive the scene of reality. A great lorry has toppled over onto a car and others have then joined the fray, unable to stop. The central reservation is breached. The road is closed to oncoming traffic and Kate's lane painfully winds its way into the other carriageway, past the dead machines, the remains of the crushed car, only just recognisable as such. The ambulances have, mercifully, pulled onto the hard shoulder, giving death a notional privacy. The driver in the car in front is straining across the passenger seat to see more out of the nearside window as he talks into his mobile with one hand and steers with the other. Beyond the police cars and machinery, civilians are huddled on the grass. *They must be super-human, the people that do this work. How do they cope? Such courage. Such humanity.*

There is a man in shock. Dazed, he is walking around, still in his suit and tie, with a blanket a paramedic has given him. Kate feels their eyes meet although surely he cannot see her behind her darkened windows. He is transformed by the blanket from citizen to victim. *Is this the future? This man is on every news broadcast, a shorthand for catastrophe.* Wherever civilisation meets the unequal threat of natural or man-made disaster : a businessman in a sharp suit and an expensive watch, with blood on his face and a blanket around his shoulders. Here he is being interviewed at Ground Zero, covered in ash; here he is in Beirut and again in Baghdad, describing the aftermath of a car bomb; here again in the wake of a suicide bomb at Athens airport, here his wet clothes cling to him and weigh him down after the *tsunami*. War, air crashes, motorway accidents, terrorist attack, natural disasters ensuing from climate change - the man in the suit and the blanket represents them all. In a variation he clasps to his chest a dead child. The blanket marks the transition from life to disaster. *And that's how long it takes. No longer than it does to throw a blanket around your shoulders.*

NINE

Wednesday afternoon 1723

PUTTING MORTALITY ONCE more behind them, the drivers pick up speed, turn up the volume of the radio and head for home with renewed urgency, their lateness now a matter for commiseration rather than blame. Half an hour later Kate turns into her village. Anxiety and hope flicker within her. They had waited years to buy a house like this, an eighteenth-century Mill House on a fine clear stretch of the Test with a chalk bed, the mill itself still intact. Kate still dreamed about a transformation of the mill itself, into what she was not sure - some sort of accommodation perhaps, a B & B? People she could make breakfast for, pick flowers for, hang pictures for. Other women, really, that is what she meant. *The boys don't really notice. Pleasing mother at last.*

The river ran through the back garden like a secret. Lawn from the river to the house, a walled garden, a tennis court, a pool over there past the yew hedge. All the trimmings, as the estate agent said. In addition to the garden, the property came with a few acres of woodland and beyond them their neighbour's fields secured the view for years to come. Kate's inheritance from her aunt had made it possible and it had felt like home to them all from the beginning. The move to the Mill House was a liberation after four years in the confines of their cottage. The boys expanded and thrived in the extra space.

Max was Kate's artistic boy, gifted at getting a likeness from an early age. Long ago he overtook her own meagre talent but still they liked to sit in the long grass together and sketch the creatures they found. Until he was about eight their was no room in Max's life for any greater love than Sebastian and then, slowly but surely, there came a diversity of looks, talents and paths which relieved Kate. *I thought my job was nearly done.* She had reckoned without the teenage years. They would return home in triumph, in love, in trouble, or in debt and still look to her for comfort. *How much love they need now.*

After meditation Kate takes her morning herb tea onto the terrace as early as she can. In Summer she craves this untouched moment of the day. No music yet streaming from the pc, no TV. Too early for the heat and stickiness of sunbathing; a day as yet unsullied by conversation or the news. At her first silent retreat, the sitting began at seven the next morning and alternated with walking meditation throughout the day. There were no chores, no telephone calls, no emails to deal with. It was a shock that she was not supposed to read. Being constantly in the company of her own internal voices was harder than she had imagined. After twenty-four hours she was suffering intensely, her restless mind aching for distraction and envying the others who seemed so untroubled by the regime. As she learned afterwards, this is not an easy time for anyone and slowly she grew to value these sojourns from her life and the strength she accrued from them. Her meditation practice at home grew steadier.

In Winter the frost first melts on this side of the house but there is a brief half hour when the sun squirts through the mist and the sparkle of rime on stone dazzles her. Shading her eyes she can still see Max and Seb, small, blond ragamuffins, kicking a ball on the lawn. Here they picknicked, barbecued, fought, swam in the river and played at fishing and boat-building. Here they invited their friends. Last week, blinking into the first light, she had imagined another small child playing there. *A girl, after all. Leila.*

Now her tall and charming twenty-year-olds hardly left the house during their university holidays, although occasionally in Summer, you might find them and their friends splashing in the pool or drying off in the sun like animals. Kate remembered her own shortlived teenage years with regret. She had not expected to see anyone playing on that lawn now until grandchildren arrived. No e.t.a. for that happy day. Instead she has started to allow herself the pleasure of imagining a child at her own breast once more, the first steps, first words, first tears of another small person whom she can sense but has not met. Billy's call drove that pleasure into hiding and sucked her into a vortex of anxiety. This December night she returns to the Mill House needing a sanctuary, wounded in a way of which she does not yet appreciate the full consequences. Six o'clock and it was properly dark as the headlights lit up the drive and the mist of the motorway gave way to the thick fog of the riverside. The gates opened and Kate's automatic swung easily around the trees and made the comforting crunch of German car on English gravel. All her life she had wanted a gravel drive, a nurturing sweep encompassing the entrance to the house. *Protection. Money. Safety.*

Billy penetrated that safety, took her to places she very much wanted to avoid. She felt a fool, now. A fool in need of sympathy and physical contact, a hot bath, a blanket around her shoulders and someone to fall asleep on. *Rob. But something is wrong; the house is in darkness.* Anonymous, gargantuan figures line the garden as fog obscures the detail of the big oaks. *There is a body on the gravel by the front door. What the hell is going on? Where are the dogs? More especially, where's Rob? Surely he must be home by now?* But his car is not there. These thoughts are so fast, she does not see or hear them come or go. How do we sense our thoughts? In the few seconds that it takes to park in front of the house Kate sees that the dead body lying outside the front door is the Christmas tree that Nigel has left her. *Shit!* If only she had spent today decorating the house. But she is not about to relax into regret. Rather, she is propelled back into energetic alertness as the emptiness of the space on the drive where Rob usually parks echoes in her body. A great void opens up in her and there is pain.

Suddenly Kate can feel all the tension she is carrying and how urgently she has been counting on putting down this burden tonight by telling her husband at last all that has happened. *And about the baby.* To discuss at last what they should do. To make her pitch for an act of faith, to make her case for Leila. *But he is not here. Oh, Christ...* Her heart makes a small internal movement which tells her she is afraid. Her stomach contracts with fear. Her mind returns to the accident on the motorway - *of course I was trying not to look* - she cannot remember anything about the car it was that they were extracting from under the pantechnicon, fallen like a giant tree in a storm. *But it was a BMW.* She saw the badge, strangely preserved in the wreckage. *Could it have been Rob's? Is that the route he would have taken?* Her heartbeats accelerate as she realises that even the colour of the car is unknown to her; there were no street lights at that fatal point and the flashing blue and yellow of the emergency services drained the policemen's faces and threw over the vehicles the effective disguise of artificial light. Even the ambulance blankets and the smears of blood on the paramedic's face are black at night. The pools on the road could as easily be oil as blood. Motorway accidents happen daily now it seems. *Why should we be spared? Did I drive past him as he took his last breath?*

She feels again the pain of watching her father die. How many times he came home from the hospital only to return by ambulance as he felt the terror and he could not breathe. She was pregnant and terrified. At the end he was unconscious and alone. *Out of pain, they said. How do they know? 'He wouldn't have known anything'.* The cars collide fatally or the morphine takes hold or the ageing body yields to its own overwhelming frailty. Kate pictures Rob grievously injured, lying on tarmac, slipping from unconscious to dead. 'He wouldn't have known anything'. *Yeah, right.*

Wednesday evening 1807

KATE HAS SWITCHED off the engine. The lights and heating have died inside the car. Her imagination has led her into trouble and beyond over the last few days. Her career at the Samaritans is in question. She questions now her own judgment, her motives. Scrupulously she tries to rationalise what she sees. *He's late, for God's sake. He's been delayed. Nothing sinister. Don't let your mind screw you up again.* Only the security light near the front door flashes an irregular warning on and off. They have never wanted the burglar alarm lifesyle many of their friends enjoy and aside from a couple of laptops, there is very little inside to attract the casual burglar. One or two good pieces of furniture, a couple of paintings. These things, the police tell her, are difficult to dispose of and traceable. *High risk for a casual thief.*

Late, and looking shifty - *have they been suborned?* - the labs materialise from the shadows and wait beside her car door. Their eyes are a dangerous yellow when the light catches them. They look wilder than usual. *I've left them for too long.* Kate hates coming home to a dark house. She unplugs her mobile from the charger and pushes open the heavy car door against wet dog.

'Hello Keeper, where were you?'

But again the fantasy has Kate in its iron grip as she remembers the crash. On the dark drive with the dogs crowding her, she snatches her mobile from her handbag once more, searching the tiny screen. *My life back, please. I'll never be naughty again. No missed calls. No messages. Just that stupid picture of Rob in a party hat that Sebastian put on there.*Kate stands on her gravel drive and drops of water gather on her hair and coat. Her face is wet. The fog is eating her alive. Is the pain in her belly part of her anxiety?

With monumental effort she walks the short distance to the front door and finds the right key. The light switch to her left is easily reached and momentarily the hall is illuminated until a small crack sounds overhead and the bulb is dead. The fuse to that light has always been a problem. *The whole ground floor dead or just that bulb?*

Standing in the hall, fighting tears of exhaustion and frustration, Kate becomes aware of the noise and in the dark, she freezes. The commonplaces of her life are transformed in her tired mind by fear and darkness. Threatening shapes furnish the hall as the unexplained bumping noise reaches her from upstairs. Her mind explores its library of sound for clarification. This particular sound is muffled knocking. *Like someone looking for something at the back of a wardrobe. In the dark. My stomach is really hurting now. It feels like labour.* She recognises the box of Christmas decorations over by the piano.The front door is open behind her and the dogs stand obediently, though not patiently, on the doorstep. They have to use the back door and they are waiting for Kate to go round and open it. The back door lies a million miles away through two darkened rooms. The stairs are ahead of her, a few paces away. The mystery noise originates, indecently, inside her sanctuary, her home. *Upstairs.*

Uncertainty makes her legs heavy, her mind slow. Meanwhile her heart races. Finally the need for light is greater than the fear and, putting her hand firmly on the banister, she walks briskly up the stairs, the reassurance of their known intervals giving her courage. On the half-landing she pauses. *I don't trust that silence.* As she moves again to climb the final three stairs, the bumping noise begins once more. No light betrays the origin of the noise. *Whatever they are doing, they are doing it in pitch darkness.* Kate feels her way towards the noise treading with painful care, straining her ears to give meaning to the sound and holding her breath. *What am I doing?* The idea of Billy has undone her sense of reality, her trust in her own judgment. She imagines him in some sort of crazy quest to meet her. *Could he get out? Could he find my house?* In her right mind these questions would have no toehold, but things are coming too thick and fast for Kate. Her mind runs over her day. The tension, the worry, the humiliation, all the energy she lost in those mock heroics, the harrowing accident, Rob not being there, the body on the drive, not knowing where he is, the light blowing. Fear has saturated her like the fog.

Wednesday evening 1815

At the top of the stairs Kate reaches a light switch; pauses. *Safer with the light on or off? I am lying in my bedroom, the one with the aeroplane wallpaper. I am five and we have not been in the house long. Still the other people's wallpaper. A pink paraffin heater with a blue flame whispers in the corner. The nightmare has passed and yet I know that any small movement, any attempt to call out for help or comfort, will make it start again. The wolf will emerge from under the bed. Annihilation is close by and only extreme stillness can delay it. I can remember now the moment at which my brain would catch up with the fact that I was awake and how my body went through a sea of pins and needles as relief dawned and I could move again. Now, I get something similar as I surface from a bad migraine.*

An intruder will be disadvantaged in the dark, not knowing the house. He won't know I'm on my own. But primeval forces are driving Kate's five-year-old fingers towards the light switch. She has a great need to see her home and her adversary, the wolf. For a moment, she is once more crouching beside Brian's bed as he dies. *Daddy.* A split-second decision illuminates the upper corridor. Kate sees nothing unusual. The noise draws her on. Directly ahead the master bedroom, the door open; off to the left a long corridor overlooking the garden one way and giving onto bedrooms the other. Her study at the far end. To the right another bedroom and bathroom, once the nursery, before Kate's time. Again the noise has stopped. Kate instinctively turns left. The noise has begun again, slightly louder now. *It is coming from my study.* The light is on and yet she is still running her hand along the wall as if she were in the dark, perhaps for moral support. Her fingertips have reached the picture of the boys taken in Italy a few years ago. In fact as she tiptoes along the seagrass carpet, she can trace her life and those of her children from Christening to Victor Ludorum along these walls. *It feels like a farewell.* Here is her favourite photograph of herself with her father. She is smiling broadly and her plaits are swinging in their red bows. *I have Daddy to myself.*

I HAVE COME straight from the airport. Daddy is dying out there in the sitting room in his favourite armchair. His favourite ashtray and the Number Six, the Swan Vestas from which he used to give me the little swans, these had long gone. I may not live any longer but it will certainly feel like it, he had said on giving up smoking and Scotch after surgery.

'His lungs are filling with water, you see,' explained the young doctor, the earnest and anonymous locum who had answered their emergency call. The young man was looking at his feet as he did when his consultant questioned him on the ward. Death did not frighten him but feelings did. *The wife is clearly on the verge of hysteria; the pregnant lady is the one to talk to.* 'The body is closing down, first the digestion, now the circulation and the breathing. There may be double incontinence to deal with.' He looks regretfully at the floor. 'Soon his body will be out of his control.' No-one expects to go like this. But death frightened Kate and almost more so the idea that her father's own body would be out of his control.

Daddy! who controlled the world! This is against nature. The doctor was wrong, of course. It was another month before life relinquished its hold on this old soldier. A massive brain haemmorhage rendered him uncontactable for the last five days of his life and Marilyn and Kate took it in turns to pace the private room in The Royal Bath Hospital. Kate read *Hamlet*. Within, Brian made his peace with God by inches and travelled the agonising *via dolorosa* alone.

Wednesday evening 1817

KATE BECOMES ACUTELY aware of the noise again. *Is this my life flashing before me?* The proximity of danger to her home, the safest place she knows, is depriving her of the will to live. A terrible apathy and depression is taking hold. *Whatever I do is useless.* Her head is full of Billy and her own stupidity. Somehow she seems to have threatened her family refuge. *Is this my own fault? I love to be right, like Mother. How often do I convince myself that what I want is right?*

The pain inside, the fear for Rob's safety, both are somehow preventing her body from preparing to deal with this immediate danger. Halfway to the study she stops again beside a small water-colour she bought on her first student trip to Venice. *Venice.* She and Rob have been promising themselves a trip alone together and the thought of this brings her strength. Determination, even courage, takes her the last yard and as she draws level with the door which is ajar, she is at last ready to fight for the chance to live the rest of her life.

But at that very moment something about the noise reaching her ear through the twilight of her study, allows her to relax. In her panic she had thought the noise entirely random, stopping and starting with the organic vigour of a person who does not have long to complete his task. *But no. I was wrong. It stops and starts predictably.* She can tell now that it is machine-made - over time a pattern emerges. There is, after all, no intruder. *There's no-one here.* Kate switches on the light and sees no-one, nothing out of place. However, the door to the printer is open, the door Kate herself left open to replace the ink cartridges. Endlessly the printer has been trying to align them; the cartridge holders whizz back and forth on the carriage, pausing, trying to force the printing into action and failing. Thus the knocking and bumping sound. She switches on the light.

Only now does she see the trail of blood which follows her from the corridor into the study. Only now does she feel the warmth and stickiness she has been trying to ignore. The evaporation of the external danger and the simultaneous disintegration of her most cherished hopes cause complex reactions within her as she looks from the soiled carpet to the printer and back again. Kate falls exhausted into her desk chair and her chest constricts with the tears which fall hot onto her hands. The fear and the relief are equally distressing; the pain sets in in earnest, now that her mind can afford to give it space. How long does she sit there? A lifetime. Leila's lifetime.

Swiftly she walks back up the corridor towards the stairs. She stops at her own bedroom and in the bathroom does what is necessary to staunch the flow of blood. Without pausing she comes back to the top of the stairs. She can see the dogs waiting with wagging tails at the front door, still open as she left it. Their yellow eyes no longer dangerous but sympathetic. Outside the fog is yellow too, reflecting back to her the lights she has put on. *Lights.* Kate finds the fuse box in the landing cupboard and pushes back down the switch. Once downstairs she shuts the front door and lets the dogs in through the kitchen, putting on all the lights as she goes. *Painkillers.* Kate takes two with a hot cup of tea with whiskey in. *The Archers* is burbling in the kitchen and she has the dogs on the rug beside her. She is safe, but her heart is broken. She puts out her hand to call Sebastian. Max is too far away.

I wouldn't tell him. No, but... Her wounds need her own attention. This is not a burden for the twins to shoulder, even unwittingly. They will both be here for Christmas in a few days. Until then she must tend to herself. *Rob.* Her mind, on a loop, keeps returning to her husband, to her own need. The vehicle she saw destroyed by the lorry on the M4, was it, after all, the dark blue BMW that he drives? The times she has wished he would slow down, not take those risks, come back to her now and feed her anxiety. The guilt she feels about Billy - what she has done and what she has failed to do - must be expiated and in her mind, no suffering seems too great. Her mind has dwelled too long on death.

Eventually she knows the time has come and she is ready to say goodbye. In her bathroom she lights candles, runs a bath, hot and deep, and pours into it oils of cinammon and nutmeg. *Domestic smells.* English smells by adoption some hundreds of years ago. She thinks of the women arriving at the tomb on Easter morning to anoint the body. *And no body was there.* Kate has no myrrh and, once again, no body to mourn over. This parting, this transition is more metaphysical. *A test of faith.* Vivaldi's Gloria is playing She lights candles and makes obeisance, though more to the mystery of life than to any particular god. At last, she steps out of her clothes and wipes from her body the blood. *The precious blood.* Beneath the ibuprofen the pain is a relief. It gives meaning to her loss. *Leila.*

That little figure on the lawn has abandoned her. She cries quietly now, her miraculous pregnancy over. Her decision permanently shelved. Her husband untouched by the joy and the grief she knows. Middle age and death await her and at this moment it seems that she must greet them in isolation. And yet, steeping in the hot, sweet water, the music lifting her into a more exquisite suffering, Kate gives thanks for the precious weeks she was permitted with her little girl and allows her to depart. *Nunc dimittis.* Sundays in Harrogate. *Evensong.* Lord, now lettest Thou Thy servant depart in peace.

Wednesday evening 1946

IT IS SHORTLY after she has dried herself and lies, wrapped in a dressing gown on top of the bed that the telephone rings. It is like waking to another life as she picks up the receiver by the bed. Rob speaks through Vivaldi of a series of disasters which have delayed him and promises to be with her within the hour. She says little. Tears again flood her cheeks.

'You weren't worried, were you, Darling? The fog...'

'A bit. No, it's OK. Things have been a bit, you know... I'll tell you when you get here. Everything's fine. Don't worry.' And yes, there is indeed some acceptance. Things may yet be fine. Kate has moved on from where she was before Billy first called. It is to be a while before her own new life takes root and blossoms within her, but the seed is there.

POSTSCRIPT

But what happened to Billy? He had a stroke of luck.

In 2004 there was a scandal at Park House when the new psychiatrist noticed that something was wrong. The more vulnerable men were often seen with injuries that were not clearly explained and only intermittently treated. An investigation was called for. The Home Secretary was involved and Sheila and Maeve were struck off the nursing register for good. The hearing found that ...

> *'The residents in Park House had an accident rate two hundred per cent higher than the national average. Record keeping had failed. Many of the inmates had suffered serious burns as a result of lack of supervision. Allegations of actual abuse by the staff remain unsubstantiated. However the Matron and her assistant had failed to ensure that vulnerable residents were not placed at risk in the kitchen or the bathroom. In addition, patients with severe behavioural difficulties were scattered randomly throughout the home and allowed to frighten and abuse the elderly residents.'*

At the hearing before the Nursing and Midwifery Council in London, it was alleged that Mrs Sheila Hardman and Miss Maeve Highsmith had run an establishment where the residents were largely overweight and sedated. They were, in the words of the report, 'sitting ducks' for any cruelties which the staff chose to heap upon them.

Sheila and Maeve refused to appear at the hearing; they vanished from the world of secure hospitals and set up a kennels at Camber Sands. They knew how to be kind to dogs. Dr Newley, now retired, was beyond the reach of the BMA. The police decided not to press criminal charges.

December 2008

FOR BILLY IT was a lucky break when Park House closed. He was transferred to a small secure unit, a mixture of men with learning disabilities and personality disorders. Here he is happily engaged in work with textiles. He has had no more accidents. A couple of the men have taken Billy under their wing and he is tolerated. This evening he is playing pool. He is no competition of course, but at last he can join in. Five of them are learning to live together here and best of all there is a befriending scheme. Billy now has a regular visit from Wilma who brings him cakes and admires the work he has done. Wilma sings in the same church choir as Iris, a widow now, who is always glad to have news of Billy. Now Harry has married and moved on, Iris may even visit one day.

'Don't tell him just yet, Wil.'

'I don't know how you can, after what he did. You're a saint, Iris,' says Wilma putting her arms around her friend.

'No, dear. I just follow my heart when I can. My duty was to Fred. I could not hurt him any more for the world, but he is at peace with Our Lord now. Who knows but He may bring me and Billy together again'.

Billy calls the Samaritans much less than he used to.

KATE STILL VISITS Marilyn, still with that apprehension in her stomach. If only she could have made things OK for her mother - but she can see that this is an internal loop of suffering, not reality. We cannot live other people's lives after all.

ROB AND KATE are still at the Mill House and there were no more children.

Kate is training to be a counsellor and Rob is at home more than he used to be. He enjoys being a success. From time to time Kate has shared her tears with Rob about her miscarriage, the little girl they did not have. To her surprise he was as sad as she herself was.

'But as long as I have you, Katie,' he says, touching her face, 'as long as you still love me..' *And I do,* thinks Kate.

Max is flying home for Christmas. He made a late start at University where he took up Chinese. The aircraft is about to take off. As he does up his safety belt and gives her hand a squeeze, he wonders if he should have told his parents he was bringing home his Chinese bride.

THE END

Printed in the United Kingdom by
Lightning Source UK Ltd., Milton Keynes
137346UK00001B/163-210/P

9 781849 232258